CW00871813

ISBN 978-0-266-73622-6
PIBN 10148878

FB &c Ltd, Dalton House, 60 Windsor Avenue, London, SW19 2RR.
Company number 08720141. Registered in England and Wales.

For support please visit www.forgottenbooks.com

IT PAYS TO ADVERTISE

BY

ROI COOPER MEGRUE
AND
WALTER HACKETT

NOVELIZED BY
SAMUEL FIELD

ILLUSTRATED WITH SCENES FROM THE PLAY

NEW YORK
GROSSET & DUNLAP
PUBLISHERS

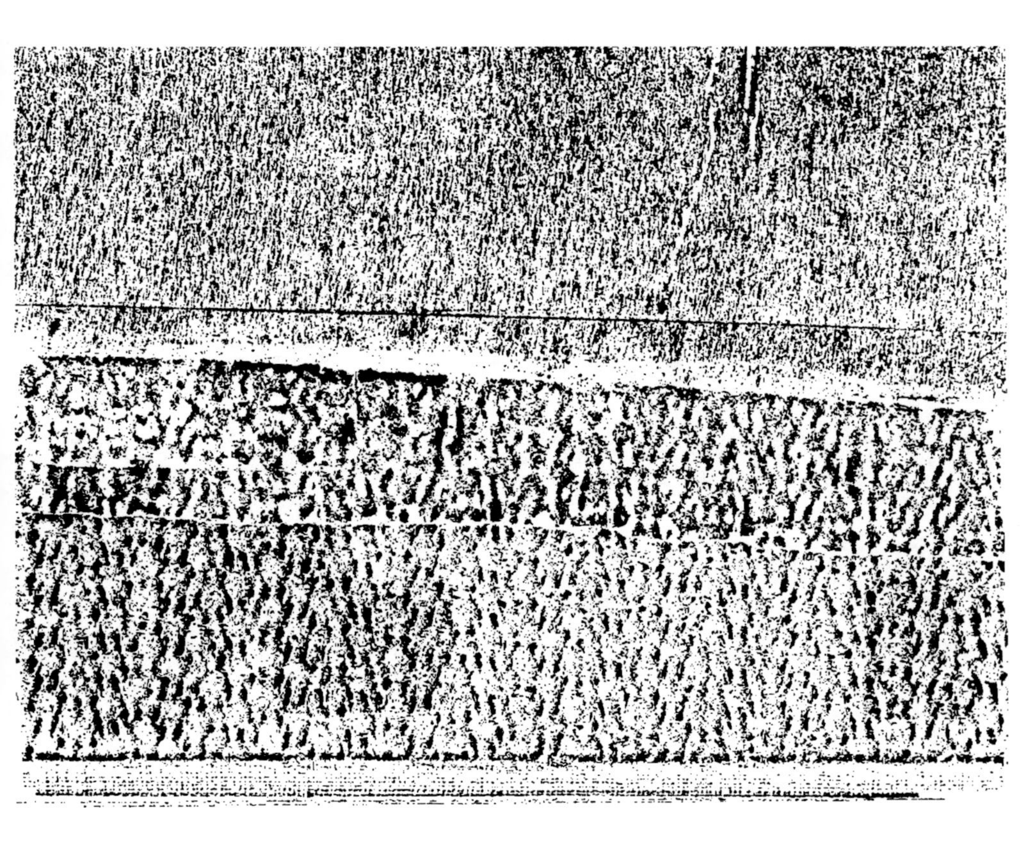

CONTENTS

LIST OF ILLUSTRATIONS

CHAPTER I

A RICH MAN'S SON

IT PAYS TO ADVERTISE

CHAPTER I

A RICH MAN'S SON

OLD CYRUS MARTIN, the soap king, sat in his library in no very contented frame of mind. There was a thorn in his flesh and he began to feel it more and more. It was not an agreeable sensation, a thorn in the flesh, for a soap king whose cuticle was not accustomed to it.

The fact was that Mr. Cyrus Martin, sixty-five years old, richer than it is wholesome for most people to be, in fairly good health, except for a touch of real or imaginary gout now and then, enjoying his semi-retirement from an old established and lucrative business, was nevertheless conscious this afternoon of a distinct subcurrent of irritation. He traced it more or less vaguely to his meeting that morning with his old friend and rival in the soap business, John Clark. They had fallen in with each other, as often happened, at the Directors' Club, about lunch time, and had one of their half friendly, half hostile chats together. And to make a long story short, Martin had bet Clark thirty thousand dollars that his son, Rodney Martin, would be making more money in a year's time than Clark's son Ellery. As neither boy had ever made a penny in his life, unless betting on a football game or winning a jackpot could be called making money, there was a fairly sporty flavor to the bargain.

The Directors' Club was one of those sumptuous rich men's lunch associations that are fairly numerous in the lower regions of Manhattan. It occupied a triad of floors in a skyscraper situate in that extremity of the Island where the East River and the North converge. From its windows, as the doughty magnates, its members, sat in the fine lounging rooms, superb views of the harbor were revealed, sharp and clear even through the haze of expensive cigars that floated lazily upward to the high ceilings. Old John Clark had come in and thrown himself into the huge cavern of a brown leather armchair near Martin's, with a cup of garnet-colored coffee in a tabouret at his elbow, and in no time at all was on his favorite topic of Ellery, that young prodigy of a son of his (in Clark's estimation) which was sure to crop up with the last two inches of his Havana. The joke of it was that Ellery's business ability was entirely a figment of the paternal imagination. To Mr. Martin, Ellery always seemed, as he used to say, "a nasty, egotistical, self-satisfied young puppy." Nevertheless the bits of business lore, and anecdotes of sagacity and trade that Clark represented as coming from the precocious lips of the marvelous Ellery had finally goaded old Martin into fury. He, at least, knew that Rodney was a nincompoop in business, if he was his son; he had no illusions about that. But the comparisons had reached a point finally beyond which he would not let them proceed unchallenged, and so he had made his ridiculous wager, and must abide by it. As he reviewed the matter in his own library, in the let-down mood of five o'clock, the memory of it all was enough to make his lunch rankle and impair digestion, a very unfortunate state of affairs for sedentary old gentlemen like retired soap kings. The prospect of turning over thirty thousand dollars to John Clark in a year's time, and admitting Rodney's incompetence to boot, was devilish.

What was the matter with rich men's sons anyway? thought Cyrus Martin. Rodney's father had not spoiled him: his father's conscience was clear on that point at least. Perhaps he had not spoiled him enough: his mother used to think so. Perhaps his mother, had she lived, with that nervous way she had of prodding people on, would have been of benefit when mere sternness had failed. Rodney's mother was the subject of occasional practical regrets such as these on her husband's part, though otherwise she was one of those formally enshrined memories before which he did not always candidly raise his eyes and read the truth. She had not been his first love, but she had been a faithful and devoted wife; she had borne him only one son and heir for all his millions, but she had brought him social distinction and rank in that vaguely defined but inescapable nobility of New York democracy. It had been her idea to send Rodney to a fashionable school. Had he not indeed been entered there at birth, with a good bit of quiet trumpeting over feminine tea-cups in the drawing-room, and tall masculine glasses at the club? And from school he had naturally gone to college, though his father could not honestly see that these four years of expensive tuition had increased his efficiency by one per cent. The boy had spent more money in college each year than the sum total of his father's and mother's expenses during the first childless years of their married life; not necessarily on fast living, his father was reasonably sure of that, but for luxuries and gewgaws at which young men in the old days would have turned up their noses. Rodney's father had not gone to college himself, though his parents could have sent him. He was not altogether a self-made man. His own father, Rodney's grandfather, a country banker in Connecticut, had left him the heritage of a modest fortune and thrifty habits, and in the soap king's mind now these seemed more to be thankful for than half a dozen college professors and their snap courses. Yet there was nothing particular the matter with Rodney's inheritance and environment; there was just something lacking in the boy himself.

Compare Rodney, for instance, with young Rufus Plodman, son of old Elihu Plodman of the Rock Rib Wire and Iron Works. Rufus was one of the liveliest young men in the business world, married to a nice wife and with a family growing up already; his name was beginning to be mentioned more and more. Then there was Chauncey Brinkhurst, who took the burden of the Excelsior National Bank almost entirely off old Brinkhurst's shoulders; and a good thing for the depositors too. There was even Will J. Robinson Jr. of the Pulver Dye Works Company, who had brought in orders that set the concern on its feet, there was good reason to believe, in just the nick of time. Compare all these and a good few others with his own young hopeful, and which name got the best of it?

What was it? Was there really something lacking in Rodney, or had he just escaped the combination that would throw open the abilities locked up in him? Old Cyrus Martin could not help chafing at the thought of Rodney going through life without definite aim or distinction. He could not bear to think of his being just a social butterfly, fluttering from one fashionable rendezvous to another, an unproductive laborer to the end. Had he not read of some young Englishman of title who had gone down in the book of fame as an amateur dancer? Heaven forbid that Rodney should live in history as a chaser of tango teas.

The boy was attractive too; his father had always liked him. Perhaps that was one of the chief troubles. Even as a little child he had never flown into tempers or had hateful ways. His own winning and non-combative disposition had been the chief means, no doubt, of warding off the disciplines of life. He was amiable and good-looking in an unobtrusive way, and everybody liked him. To look at him impartially you would not have thought he lacked character, unless you yielded too much to your prejudice against a slight lisp and an otherwise somewhat finicky way of talking. He did not run into debt now, or overdraw his allowance, or at any rate not very much;

he had never done so much, and in college he had got fairly good marks, as nearly as his father could make out, and had won his degree of A. B. without too obvious difficulty. Didn't the precious sheepskin hang framed on the wall of his room, surrounded by a veritable picture gallery of college glee clubs and elevens and nines? Cyrus Martin had been credibly informed that you could not actually graduate from Harvard or Yale or Princeton without some portion of mentality. Where did it show itself in Rodney? As a boy he had had his flashes of cleverness and wit; what propensity had been revealed in them? Ransacking his memories, old Martin could not remember what they were; had they been merely the subjective readings of fond parents' minds? Why was Rodney so different from old Clark's boy Ellery?

Well, perhaps Clark was a good deal of a bluffer in this instance. Martin must call the bluff and win out somehow in the matter of this bet, or his life would not be worth living.

He rang the bell sharply for Johnson, his butler, prepared to have a pretty sharp twinge of gout if the summons was not promptly answered.

"Any one call this afternoon, Johnson?" he asked, when that silent-footed dignitary appeared.

Johnson took a silver tray from the table near

the hall door and glanced downward at it stiffly.

"The Countess de Beaurien," he said, impassively.

"Who the Devil's she?" asked Mr. Martin.

"I don't know, sir. She couldn't speak a word of anything but French. Marie was off to-day, sir, and nobody else could get anything out of her. She claims she had a letter of introduction to you from your Paris partner, Monsieur Rivard."

"Has Rivard lost his mind?" muttered Martin. "Was she old or young or pretty or what?"

"I couldn't say, sir. You can't sometimes always tell with them French ladies, sir."

"A letter from Rivard?" muttered Martin. "I don't believe it. He's never given any one a letter to me without tipping me off. Johnson, hand me that fat red book in the lower right hand corner there."

Johnson stooped obediently and extracted an Almanach de Gotha from the revolving bookcase. Mr. Martin took it and began turning over the leaves rapidly, observing as he did so:

"You know, Johnson, it's easier to read French than speak it."

"So I understand, sir," returned the butler.

"Beauclair, Beauvale — oh, here she is, Beaurien. No, she is not. A fake, Johnson, just as

I supposed. The Countess de Beaurien is seventy years old, and at her death the title becomes extinct. Was the lady this afternoon as old as seventy, Johnson?"

"Oh no, sir. Not at all, sir."

"Are you sure she asked for me and not Mr. Rodney?"

"Quite sure, sir. Miss Grayson was here, sir, and can tell you. We had a time of it."

"Some lady going into business to do America or the Americans," was Mr. Martin's inward comment. "Anybody else?" he added aloud.

"Yes, sir," said Johnson. "Mrs. Cheysemore. She left the blank for the Y.M.C.A. subscription."

"I hope you remember that I'm always out for her, Johnson."

"Yes, sir. I know, sir."

Mr. Martin thought it really a little shameful how many times this pious lady came to see him, and he was a bit ashamed too for the whole modern female sex to think how many others, her contemporaries, and at least her equals in looks, original or restored, would set their caps for an old widower like himself if they received the slightest encouragement. Some of them did not wait for the encouragement, of whom Mrs. Cheysemore was one, and they were religiously kept upon the out list by the redoubtable Johnson.

"And who else? Give me that tray."

Mr. Martin took the salver and peered beneath the rims of his glasses at the bits of pasteboard. "Ambrose Peale," he read. "Press representative: Belle of Broadway Company."

"Now who was that, Johnson?"

"He was calling on Mr. Rodney, sir," said Johnson. "He's been here several times, but never left his card before."

A press agent from a Broadway show after Rodney? The young man's father groaned inwardly. Oh Lord, he thought, what next! Visions of breach of promise, of black bird dinners, or even elopements, flashed through his mind. This settled it. Rodney simply must be anchored somehow.

"Is Mr. Rodney in, Johnson?" was the next inquiry.

"No, sir. Not now, sir."

"Do you know where he is now?"

"From one to two he was at the Knickerbocker at lunch, sir. From two thirty to three he was at Farrell's looking at a new hunter, sir. From four to five he's at the Raquet Club, sir."

"Good heavens, Johnson, how do you know all that?" exclaimed Mr. Martin.

"Because he left the telephone numbers, sir,

and I was to let him know if Miss Grayson came in, sir."

"And has she been here, Miss Grayson?"

"Yes, sir, she's been here since four o'clock, sir, doing some typing. She's still waiting for you."

"Why the devil didn't you say so, then?"

"I was coming to her presently, sir."

"Tell her to come in, then, to the library. And, Johnson, don't you bother to ring up and tell Mr. Rodney anything, do you understand?"

"Yes, sir. Nothing, sir."

It was really faithless of Johnson, the soap king thought, to betray Rodney's well-laid plans, but Rodney's father had plans of his own in frustrating them. Let that silly ass Johnson think what he had a mind to: he didn't want Mary Grayson for himself, and he didn't care if she was poor. She came of good stock — he had known her mother — and there could be many a worse fate for Rodney than being caught in her net. He was not sure, in point of fact, if the girl wasn't spreading her nets quietly. The old man was a shrewd judge of character, and there was an idea taking shape in the back of his mind that Mary Grayson might help him earn that thirty thousand dollars.

His library was a large square room, the whole

width of the house and as many feet deep. The walls were lined with tapestries, and behind the leaded glass of the dark oak bookcases were many rows of leather bound volumes, not all of which the soap man pretended to have read. A fire of well dried wood burned brightly in the grate, for the September day had turned very cool, and a clock from Tiffany's ticked and swung its diamond studded pendulum on the mantelpiece between the symmetrical candlesticks that flanked it on either side. Through the heavy curtains the rays of the setting sun came into the room across the Park, and the screeching of a motor bus every now and then drowned the ticking clock and the crackling wood. Old Martin sat and thought.

Mary Grayson! Well, what made young men work? Love, sometimes, and poverty and necessity. The first might stir Rodney up, if not the second and third. But why not all three?

"She stoops to conquer," he muttered to himself. To tell the truth he had heard this phrase all his life without really taking in the meaning of it. Now he had seen the old farce comedy prettily played not long ago, and the hackneyed title of it had been ringing in his ears with rather a new meaning. Rodney might be made to stoop to be conquered — to conquer himself and his laziness of a rich man's son. On Mary Grayson's part it was not really stooping if you considered Rodney's mentality and character; he admitted it sourly. If Rodney could find an incentive in Mary Grayson, the stenographer, what did old man Martin care? He knew her for a good girl, as she was a pretty one, and nicer in speech and manners than some of the widows who made heavy eyes at him from the windows of their limousines. Lots of old fellows, he thought, might feel like making up to Mary themselves; and why not? Well, one reason for Cyrus Martin was that he had known her mother. Besides —

"Did you want me, Mr. Martin?" said Miss Grayson quietly, interrupting his revery.

CHAPTER II

A POOR MAN'S DAUGHTER

CHAPTE

A POOR MAN'S

MISS MARY GRAE
her name. She
too full of merry
like, her dazzling teeth,
her well-bred figure and
a whole that old Martin
inward breathing of
the minor economic
managed to dress so well
pay. There was no
at all; she was too clever
like her demeanour, were
and appropriate to her
that excellent thing in woman,
space, a sweet voice, and
other excellent thing in woman
Martin, a good manager.
at her now with a sigh.

"Well, how are you
he said aloud.

"Very well indeed, thank

CHAPTER II

A POOR MAN'S DAUGHTER

MISS MARY GRAYSON was as pretty as her name. Her big round eyes, that were too full of merry shrewdness to be merely doll-like, her dazzling teeth, her clear and rosy skin, her well-bred figure and way of dressing, made up a whole that old Martin never saw without some inward breathing of contentment. It was one of the minor economic mysteries of existence how she managed to dress so well on her stenographer's pay. There was no note of extravagance in it, at all; she was too clever for that. Her clothes, like her demeanor, were just modestly well bred and appropriate to her condition in life. She had that excellent thing in woman, according to Shakespeare, a sweet voice, and she was probably that other excellent thing in woman, according to Cyrus Martin, a good manager. Old Martin looked up at her now with a sigh.

"Well, how are you to-day, Mistress Mary?" he said aloud.

"Very well indeed, thank you, Mr. Martin.

I'm always well," said Miss Grayson. "Have you any letters for me to-day?"

They had gotten into the way for the last six weeks or so of having her come up to the house occasionally, when Mr. Martin did not feel equal to going to the office. He could not have been quite sure who had made the suggestion originally; he had never really given in to his gout before she came; he salved his conscience by attributing the idea to Mary, for it was an arrangement which even now the soap king never executed without a slightly guilty feeling. There is no greater punishment for a healthy business man of sixty-five than his periods of enforced leisure. His absences from the office, where everybody else is probably shirking work, are a long drawn out infliction visited upon him for his sins. Mary Grayson, with her brisk pretty ways, and her pencil poised above her stenographic pad, brought back a sense of activity and efficiency to the soap king.

"Yes, a few. But there's no hurry," he answered presently, tasting the joys and irritations of his business letters in prospect a bit.

"Oh, by the way, Miss Grayson," he went on, "Johnson tells me you were here when that Countess called this afternoon. What did you make of her?"

"Nothing, I'm sorry to say, Mr. Martin," replied Mary, laughing. "It was really too funny. I feel, as Johnson said, that my education has been neglected. 'I regret that I was not better educated, ma'am,' he said to me."

Mary went on in imitation of Johnson's inimitable manner. "'Nothing like this has ever happened to me before, Miss, but I can't make her comprehend anything I say. She just sits and waits.'"

"What was she like?" demanded Mr. Martin, laughing too, then checking himself as his fears with respect to Rodney and some designing female came back to him.

"Well, she was really rather fascinating," Mary began, taking her cue from this encouragement. "And stunning, too. The French always are, don't you think? And she had on a duck of a dress. She walked straight in and looked straight at me, and began to jabber like a streak of lightning. She never made a movement, just stood with her hands on the handle of her umbrella, while the French fairly flew out of her mouth. I told her it was impossible for her to see Mr. Martin — that he was confined to the house by a severe attack of gout, and couldn't she leave her message?"

"And did she?"

"Well, her message sounded something like this:

"'*Jedesireparleramonsieurmartinaproposdes*AFFAIRES. *Jesuisrichemaisonpeuttoujoursetreplus*RICHE. *Sijepouvaisobtenirleagencedusavonmartinpourlafrancecaseraiunebelle*AFFAIRE. *Jedonneraicinquantemillefrancspour cette*AGENCE. . . .'"

Mr. Martin's mouth fell open with amused astonishment during this tirade. He had once met a young woman who could make a noise like Sara Bernhardt, without knowing more than half-a-dozen words of French. But Mary Grayson beat her.

"Well, well," laughed Mr. Martin; "it's a wonderful language, French."

"Isn't it," said Mary. "So finally we tried signs and pantomime. I made a wild, sweeping gesture at her to show that you were out. She rattled on worse than before. Then I pretended Johnson was you, Mr. Martin, and I shoved him out of the door, and shrieked 'out!' Sometimes if you talk loud enough it seems as if they might understand you, but this one didn't. And then she began to act at Johnson and me too. She evidently wanted to know when you'd be back. She walked to the door, and we thought she was departing at last. But she came back again at once, and our hearts sank. I caught something about 'quelle

"Quite right," said Mr. Martin; "do you think she was after Rodney?"

heure' and 'rentrera-t-il,' and she took her watch out and waved it at me. So I made up my mind she wanted to know at what hour you'd reënter, so to speak; whereupon I ran over to the clock and pointed violently to the figure eight. I hope I may be forgiven for the white lie."

"Forgiven so far as I am concerned," said Mr. Martin genially. He encouraged Mary sometimes to rehearse the little incidents of the day, because she did them well, and he liked to watch her.

"I told Johnson never to let her in again unless Marie was here to interpret her," said Mary in conclusion.

"Quite right," said Mr. Martin. "By the way," he added, eyeing his pretty secretary shrewdly, "do you think she was after Rodney? Was she young enough for that?"

Mary went back to her chair and began preening her feathers and fingering her pad and pencil with a demure look that she could assume at will.

"Some women are never too old for that, are they, Mr. Martin?" she said coolly.

He glanced at her furtively a moment, as she patted back her hair, looking pleasantly at the crackling fire. There had been a time in those early days, when she had first come to him, to try her hand at a secretaryship, when she had reminded him alternately of her two parents. It was in loyalty to one of them that he had given her a chance. Sometimes, in a flash, there would be a curiously vivid suggestion of her mother in her — something in the way she raised her head and looked at him, a sound in the tone of her voice as she said good morning. Such moments, for a long time, gave old Martin a sharp pang that he could not ignore even in his inmost heart. Then there was that even sharper twinge, and a curiously less pleasant one, when she reminded him of her father: he had been a handsome dog in his day, Rob Grayson — there was no denying that. Old Martin hoped, and as he knew Mary better he began to believe and be sure of it, that the girl had got nothing from her father but his regular features and his pleasant personality. Her narration of the visit of the Countess had suggested her father, who was a capital mimic. Well, Rob had had his good points too. Probably after all the combination of the two strains had been a successful one, thought old Cyrus, with some dim notion of this new fad they called eugenics floating through his mind. But the time had long ago arrived when Mary had developed into just herself, a successful blend that had its own the proper way, thought old Cyrus. Maybe she could be made to. care, or did already. Rodney was not unattractive to women, by all accounts. An idea was taking shape in Mr. Martin's brain-pan; — if only he could put it over.

"Well, if you're ready, my dear, here goes," he began briskly.

"To John Clark, Esq.
"Ivory Soap Works,
"New York, N. Y.
"Dear Sir:

"Confirming our conversation of even date I send you a line to record the bet made this morning between us in re our sons, Ellery Clark and Rodney Martin respectively; namely, that if my boy, by his own unaided efforts, isn't making more money at the end of a year from November 1 next than your boy makes, I pay you thirty thousand dollars ($30,000.00) in cash; and if he is, then you pay that sum to me; the books of their several business concerns, duly audited, to be the deciding factor.

"Yours very truly,——

"Got that?" he added, darting a keen glance at Mary beneath his thick eyebrows.

"Yes, Mr. Martin," said that young lady, in

a voice which she was evidently trying to make as colorless as possible.

"Well, what do you think of it?" demanded Mr. Martin, breaking a short pause.

"I think Mr. Rodney has more brains than you give him credit for," said Mary impulsively.

"Oh, you do, do you?"

"Yes, sir, I do. But isn't thirty thousand dollars a good deal of money to lose on a bet? Somebody always loses, you know. And Mr. Rodney has never had any business experience to speak of. You wouldn't have him in your own works, you know."

"Of course I wouldn't. I didn't want Rod posing there as the boss's son, interfering with the good discipline of the establishment. Besides, I didn't want them all down there to see what a nincompoop he was in business. I've got more pride than that."

"Aren't you a little hard on Rodney, Mr. Martin?" asked Mary gently.

"Are you a little sweet on Rodney, Miss Mary?" retorted the soap king gruffly.

She had her head bent over her work, and he couldn't see her features during this colloquy. He would have to carry the plummet line a little deeper.

"Because if you are," he went on, "I warn

you, you'll have to marry him for love. He'll get no money from me unless he makes good. I shall make a will leaving him only an annuity, the principal to go to charity when he has idled himself into his grave. And I'll see to it that the annuity isn't quite enough for two, let me tell you, let alone a family of kids. I don't propose to have him, or a lot of worthless grandbrats, making ducks and drakes of my money when I'm gone."

"I see," said Miss Grayson demurely. "Of course it's none of my business. Anything else, sir?"

A motor bus, screeching along outside, came to a full stop at the corner. Mr. Martin, who had begun to pace the room as he talked, forgetting his convenient or inconvenient gout, lingered at the window, and saw two women alight and stand talking indefinitely on the sidewalk. In one of the windowpanes where the curtains darkened it and made a mirror, he could see Mary's pretty head drooping a little, giving her body a suddenly pensive air as she gazed abstractedly into the dying fire. He turned and spoke again and was pleased to see that she started involuntarily.

"Would you mind ringing for Johnson, my dear?" he asked, more pleasantly.

Mary rose and pressed the button, and then

sat down again as before. Johnson came presently, and obediently replenished the fire, while Cyrus Martin twiddled his keys and small change in his trousers pockets. When Johnson's stiff back had disappeared through the doorway he began again on another tack.

"Look here, Mary," he demanded, in a franker tone; "I want your help. You can help me if you will. And if you benefit by it yourself, why so much the better. Pitch in and catch Rodney, if you want him. I should be glad of it. Only there would be one condition."

Beneath this direct attack the girl did finally blush a little. She gathered herself together again, however, and folded up her book by way of recapturing her composure.

"Why, Mr. Martin," she said, "what an idea!"

"Why is it such an idea? Is there nothing to attract a young fellow and a good-looking girl like you to each other? You're too modest, Miss Mary."

"I'm not a judge of that, Mr. Martin," said Mary.

"Oh, yes, you are," retorted her employer; "and I'm not so sure you're not quite willing, myself."

"But I think you're very unkind to me," protested Mary, taking another cue. "You appeal to my woman's curiosity. Supposing, for the sake of argument, that your son and I are madly in love with each other, what are your conditions?"

"Well," said her employer, "I tell you frankly, I don't want to lose that thirty thousand dollars to John Clark, and I do want to stir Rodney up. He needs an incentive, and I've been ransacking my brains to find the right one. And I think I've found it. I think it's you."

"I, Mr. Martin? Do you really think so?" she expostulated demurely.

"Yes, I do really think so, Miss Grayson," he mimicked.

"Don't you think it's just perversity?" persisted Mary. "Do you think Rodney would really care about me if he could have me just for the asking? I don't see how I can help you at all, Mr. Martin."

"Oh, yes, you can, and I'll tell you just how," went on old Martin trenchantly. "I want Rodney to work for his money and his wife together. I'm going to turn him out of here —"

"Turn him out, Mr. Martin? Whatever do you mean?"

"Just what I say; turn him out, throw him overboard. Didn't you ever hear of the old admiral who taught his children to swim by throwing them overboard? The girls as well as the boys. If they didn't drown they swam, he said. But they usually swam!"

"But they might have drowned," objected Mary with a pretty shudder.

"No," said old Cyrus with a villain's chuckle, "I've got it all doped out. I'll turn him out, right enough. I'll find a good excuse for it. I'm mad enough with him half the time. Look here, Mary, has Rodney proposed to you yet?"

"Well, really, Mr. Martin," stammered the secretary, "do you really think —"

"Well, the next time he proposes, you're to accept him. See? You're to tell him you'll have him if his father consents, and then send him to ask me. That'll be my big scene."

"You'll say yes — you'll refuse?" stuttered Mary, showing some concern in the success of the plot, despite her efforts to be detached and business-like.

"Consent? No! That's my cue for turning him out of my house forever," roared the stage father, working himself up into quite an advanced condition of parental fury. "Let him marry a typewriter? (Don't let that hurt your feelings, my dear.) Let some designing woman get her hands on him for a rich man's son? (Business of indignation, my dear.) I'll turn him down and out in proper fashion. Upon my word I feel like doing it this minute."

"But there's one chance you've overlooked, Mr. Martin," resumed Mary, pursing her pretty mouth slightly at the corners.

"What's that?"

"That he may not propose to me again — I mean at all," she corrected.

"Well, then, I'll disinherit him for sure," roared the soap king. "Now be off with you too, before I lose my temper."

But as Mary turned to go he called after her again: — what a flat pretty back she had, he thought, subconsciously, as he watched her lay her hand on the door knob:

"No, don't go yet. There's one thing more. We must make a bona fide deal of this thing. You want to hear my terms, of course, don't you?"

"Your terms?"

"Yes, terms: and here they are. You needn't expect anything better: I'll pay you twenty-five hundred dollars down if you turn the trick. Twenty-five hundred dollars! You could use it, I suppose, couldn't you?"

At these "terms" Mary turned all the way round and leaned her pretty back against the dark mahogany door, her figure in its gray dress prettily outlined against it, and her hand still clinging to the cut-glass knob. Twenty-five hundred dollars! Twenty-five hundred dollars from Mr. Martin! Her face and eyes, if not her lips, repeated the fat and racy words. But could she? fluttered from her pretty eyes. And yet she would, said the set mouth and chin. But no, she couldn't, said her shell-like ears, blushing as pink as coral. But yes, why not, said the firm mouth at last; and Mr. Cyrus Martin, watching this delicate by-play across her lovely features, that found more favor in his sight than ever this minute, despite his gruff demeanor, knew that the fates were playing on his side.

"Very well, Mr. Martin," said Mary Grayson finally; "it's a bargain then."

"A bargain," said old Cyrus, chuckling inwardly, and rubbing his hands together like an old fashioned actor doing the part of Shylock. "Come here, and I'll give you my blessing."

He stooped and kissed her respectfully on her white forehead, and could not resist the temptation to let his hand linger a moment on the firm roundness of her upper arm and shoulder before he released her. "A bargain," he resumed, with suddenly returning gruffness. "So now go to it."

CHAPTER III

THE COURSE OF TRUE LOVE

CHAPTER III

THE COURSE OF TRUE LOVE

RODNEY MARTIN himself, as luck would have it, opened the front door with his pass key and came in just as Mary was descending into the lower hall from his father's library.

"Mary!" he exclaimed delightedly. "You here? What in thunder's the matter with Johnson?"

"One question at a time, please," said Mary, collecting herself as rapidly as possible. "What's Johnson got to do with it?"

"Why, I left my telephone numbers with him," explained Rodney; "so he could call me up the very moment you came in."

"You sound like a doctor going to the theater," said Mary.

"Same principle," echoed Rodney; "S.O.S.; C.Q.D., and all the rest of it. Safety first, you know."

Mary parried and fenced as best she could; this was going to be a somewhat earlier opportunity of putting through their scheme than she had bargained for with the old magnate upstairs. Rodney showed only too plainly that he had something on his mind. He drew her into a small reception room on the first floor, and made her sit down. It was a little pink and gold room which was never used except for a cloak room when dinners were given, or the housekeeper engaged a new servant. Lately Mary's typewriting machine had come to figure incongruously as a part of its furnishings, since the clicking keys bothered Mr. Martin in his library, and Mary came down here often to write.

Despite her bargain with the old gentleman upstairs she made a brave attempt to ward off something that she saw was inevitable, here and now. She took the lines in her own hand, and tried to steer the conversational craft safely through the rapids.

"Rodney," she said, "tell me what you have been doing to-day."

He told her.

"Well, I call that a very unprofitable twelve hours," said Mary firmly. "Rodney, why don't you do something worth while, why don't you go into some business? Have an office with your name on the door. Be somebody. It would please your father so."

Rodney was dressed in the correctest masculine

fashion, Mary noted — gray spats, a braided English morning coat, a huge white carnation in his buttonhole, and quite heavenly trousers. He wore a tie from Charvet's. Rodney was a nice boy, and had nice manners. He was only twenty-four, and his face had a certain quaint, frank charm in spite of his funny little mustache. He was by no means brainless, Mary was sure, notwithstanding his father's theories; only undeveloped by reason of the kind of life he had led, and its appallingly frictionless conditions.

At the present moment he had an unaccustomed air of resolution that pervaded all the little room, and made Mary retreat behind the typewriting desk, quailing in spite of herself. As she sat down, to her astonishment, she beheld Rodney turning the key in the door that led into the hall. The room became thus a cul-de-sac, and her exit was barred, unless she should scream to a policeman through the window. But of course she couldn't do that; and besides she suddenly remembered the twenty-five hundred dollars. Was she earning it easily, or with shocking difficulty? She could not have told you. Aloud she said:

"Why, Mr. Martin, what are you doing?"

"I want to talk to you," said Rodney, coming towards her. "I've been wanting this opportunity for days, and now that I've got it, I don't propose to be interrupted. That's why I locked the door."

Mary's little brain worked like lightning. Well, she must accept the challenge now, it seemed. Her business manner, as she sometimes called it, disappeared. Instead she assumed the fluttering airs of a timid ingenue, overdoing it, she feared in her trepidation, for any one but a boy as madly in love with her as Rodney was. Mary may or may not have heard of the paradox about acting promulgated by the famous Diderot, a compatriot of her French countess of that afternoon; — namely, that you acted best when you were completely yourself, and not when you emotionally lost yourself in your acted part. As Rodney went on, Mary, when she thought of the twenty-five hundred dollars, every now and then, unconsciously followed the school of Diderot; later she could not have certified which method guided her through her scene.

Rodney had come over to her, and now stood facing her, his eyes eager and full of light.

"I want to talk to you," he said impetuously. "Mary, will you marry me?"

"Why, really," began Mary shyly, looking sidewise and enjoying herself curiously well.

"You love me, don't you?" queried the boy warmly.

"I don't know what to say," hesitated the girl, feeling her ground.

"Say yes," cried Rodney, waiting feverishly to hear her answer.

It came at last shyly, "Yes," whereupon Rodney cried, "You angel," joyfully, and tried to grab her. But things must not go quite so fast, Mary thought intuitively, and drew away a little from him, though to tell the truth she would willingly have let him catch her, as she felt now.

"No, no; wait a moment," she said, eluding him.

"We'll be married right away," went on Rodney unabashed.

"But suppose your father disapproves," said Mary.

"He won't know anything about it until we're married — and then what could he do?" objected Rodney.

"He might cut you off," suggested Mary sagely.

"Would you care?" asked Rodney.

"I? No, no, indeed," said Mary hastily. "I was thinking of you, dear."

"Don't you bother about me," cried Rodney. "We'll be married to-morrow, and then come home for the parental blessing."

"No, I couldn't do that," said Mary. "It

wouldn't be right. I'm his private secretary. He trusts me, and brings me here to his home, and then to find I'd married his son on the sly — No, Rodney, we couldn't do that."

"You do make it sound rather bad," said Rodney. "I shouldn't want to treat father badly. We've always been pretty good friends, he and I. I guess I'd better tell him — in a week or so —"

Mary's self composure had been rapidly returning during this colloquy, and she was surer of what she wanted. Indeed it piqued her a little that Rodney should have made such a proposal to her, so that now her own inclinations and the old gentleman's upstairs ran in the same channel. She spoke up quite resolutely:

"Why, Rodney, if you love me, you will want to get this awful suspense over with."

"But suppose he does object?" Rodney argued, seeing his light of happiness grow dim.

"Even then I wouldn't give you up," said his sweetheart.

"Mary!"

"You could go into business," she went on; "make a big man of yourself; make me proud of you —"

"You talk just like the heroine in a play I saw last night," protested Rodney. "She wanted the hero to go to work, and he did, and then for four acts everybody suffered."

"Don't you want to work?" asked Mary anxiously.

"I should say not," Rodney answered quite seriously. "Imagine going to bed every night, knowing you'd got to get up in the morning and go to business."

"You'd be happier, wouldn't you?" queried Mary, "if you had a job?"

"Please don't talk like father," protested Rodney. "He's preached a job at me ever since I left college. Why should I work? Father made millions out of soap, and is forever complaining that he's always had his nose to the grindstone, that he's never known what fun was, that it's all made him old before his time. I can't see the sense of following an example like that — I really can't. He's got enough for you and me and our children and their grandchildren. I've explained all this to him, but I can't seem to make him understand. But it's simple — why work when there's millions in the family? And why even talk of it, when you and I are in love?"

He leaned hungrily toward her, stretching out his arms to her, and finished on a note of genuine appeal: "Come, kiss me, Mary."

But Mary drew back from him quickly. "No, you mustn't," she said firmly. "Not till you've spoken to your father."

"You won't even kiss me till I tell him?"

"No."

"And you will when I do?"

"Yes."

"Then I'll tell him right away," cried the valiant lover, striding to the door.

"Oh, Rodney, you're splendid," applauded Mary, "and don't be afraid."

"Afraid!" echoed Rodney scornfully. But he paused a moment at the door and said:

"You don't think I'd better wait till the morning?"

"No, I don't," said Mary; "and don't be silly about his gout. He really is a very patient invalid."

Rodney stood a moment with his hand on the knob, plucking up resolution. As he lingered there, a violent knocking sounded on the other side, and his father's voice could be distinctly heard crying "Ouch" in an extra loud tone in the hall.

"Speaking of the patient invalid," whispered Rodney, looking back at the girl for whom he was so greatly daring.

"If you don't ask him now I'll never marry,

you," whispered Mary, forming her words as distinctly as was possible under the circumstances.

"Open the door," cried the elder Martin angrily in the hall.

"I'm coming, father. Coming," quaked Rodney, as he turned the key.

The door was no sooner opened than his father strode into the room sternly, uttering the ejaculation "Ouch" twice, and the polite phrase "the devil," at least once as he crossed the threshold.

"Why was that door locked?" he demanded, scowling.

"Was it locked?" asked Rodney innocently.

"You young fool, didn't you just unlock it?" roared his father.

"So I did," said Rodney nervously.

Mary in the meanwhile had retreated to her typewriter, and now began typing violently.

"Stop that noise," shouted Mr. Martin.

The noise ceased immediately, and Rodney looked at her discouraged. She motioned to him to go on. Meanwhile Martin painfully limped to a chair by a small table and sank into it, his foot giving him another twinge.

"Ouch! Oh, my poor foot!" he moaned.

Rodney hastily picked up a footstool and came with it to his father.

"I'm afraid your foot hurts," he ventured propitiatingly.

"Not at all — I just pretend that it does," growled his father.

"I hoped you were better," said the son sincerely.

"Well, I'm not. What's that you got there?"

"A footstool — I thought it might make you more comfortable."

"Comfortable? How much do you want out of me now?" his father asked shrewdly.

"Why nothing, father," Rodney answered.

"Well, anyhow the answer is, not a nickel —"

"You do me an injustice," protested Rodney, "I'm just sorry to see you in pain."

"Well, you want something — that's certain —"

"Why do you say that?" Rodney quavered.

"I know you — and whatever it is you can't have it."

Rodney turned appealingly to Mary, who ignored him. He turned back to his father again, and tried to muster up his courage to the sticking point.

"Well, as a matter of fact, I did want —" he began, clearing his throat.

"Oh! Now we're getting to it," Martin retorted. "Well, what is it?"

"I wanted to have a talk with you — an important talk —"

"Curious! That's just what I wanted to have with you. I've wanted it all day. And now we'll have it — Miss Grayson!" he called to Mary.

"Yes, sir," said Mary meekly.

"Get out!"

She went without a glance at Rodney, who stood looking after her dejectedly, not knowing that his love's intention was to give him moral support by listening in the hall.

"Now what do you mean by overdrawing your allowance again?" she heard Mr. Martin say, when the door was closed.

"Why," innocently answered Rodney, "it simply proves that I was right when I told you my allowance was too small."

"What!" ejaculated his father, quite evidently aghast.

"And if my allowance is too small for one, it's much too small for two," the boy continued ingeniously.

"For two?"

"Father, has it ever occurred to you that I might marry?" inquired Rodney.

"Of course it has. You're fool enough for anything," growled his father.

"I don't consider a man a fool because he's married," said Rodney.

"That's because you've never tried it."

"I intend to try it, just the same," said Rodney.

"Oh, you do, do you? Who is the girl?"

"The girl?" repeated his son nervously.

"Yes, girl. You're not going to marry an automobile, or a polo pony, or an aëroplane, or any other of your idiotic amusements, are you? You're going to marry a girl, aren't you? Some blue-eyed, doll-faced, gurgling, fluttering little fool. Oh, why doesn't God give young men some sense about women?"

"I object very strongly to your speaking in that way of Miss Grayson," spoke up Rodney angrily.

"Miss Grayson? Miss Grayson — you're not going to marry a typewriter?"

"Yes, sir."

"Does she know it?"

"Yes, sir."

"Oh! Of course she knows a good thing like you when she sees it —"

"I won't listen to you talk of Miss Grayson in that way —"

"You've got to listen. I won't permit any

such absurd ridiculous marriage. Thank Heaven you had sense enough not to elope—"

"I wanted to, but she wouldn't. She insisted on your being told; so you see what an injustice—"

"Injustice—can't you see she wanted me to know so that if I disapproved and cut you off, she'd not be stuck with you on her hands?"

"Please, father—" pleaded Rodney; and then dropped his hands at his sides and turned to go, adding, "It's quite useless."

"No, my boy. Wait a minute," said Mr. Martin. "Remember I'm your friend, even if I am your father. Don't you believe it. It's only your money she wants."

"I know it isn't," replied Rodney proudly.

"I'll prove it is," said his father, pushing an enameled electric bell that stood near him on the table.

"What are you going to do?" cried Rodney nervously.

"Send for Miss Grayson," said his father grimly. "I'll tell that scheming secretary that if you persist in this marriage I'll disinherit you, and then you watch her throw you over," he amplified for Rodney's benefit.

"Even if you are my father, you shan't insult the girl I love," protested Rodney hotly.

"Poppycock! You're afraid to put her to the test. You're afraid she will chuck you," retorted his father.

But Rodney answered quietly: "I'm not afraid, father. You're mistaken."

Johnson appeared meanwhile in answer to the bell, and in a surprisingly short time, and with a queer look on his usually imperturbable face, if they had only noticed it, returned with Mary Grayson under his escort. Mary looked from father to son with an elaborately assumed air of innocence, and inquired:

"You wanted me, Mr. Martin?"

She saw Rodney, out of the tail of her eye, make a movement toward her and say, "Mary," in a pleading tone, then heard his father interrupting him curtly. "My precious son," he told her, "has just informed me that you and he intend to get married. Is that right?"

"Oh, sir," she began timidly, almost losing her composure a moment, to think of the pass that things had come to with her connivance. She was not sure, moreover, if the soap king had not really been in earnest in his fulminations as they floated out to her in the hall. Either his acting or his gout must be genuine to-day, she began to fear.

"Because I wish to tell you," he began again,

" that if he marries you he'll not get one penny of my money. And that means he'll starve. I suppose you realize that?"

Mary turned to Rodney, who was standing up very straight near the window looking on Fifth Avenue, one hand catching the braided lapel of his coat, as his eyes devoured her with such real love and confidence showing on his face that she could not resist his love's appeal to her. She took in all this, and even, with curious distinctness, noticed that the white flower in his coat had fallen loose a little, as she turned to his father and answered him courageously:

" Then at least we'll starve together."

She was rewarded by the exultation in Rodney's voice as he exclaimed, " Mary!"

" You see, father," he added, for the old gentleman's benefit.

" Making a grand-stand play, eh," went on the soap magnate remorselessly to Mary, " before my idiot of a son. You think I'm so fond of him that I'll relent. Well, you're wrong. Neither of you will ever get a nickel out of me."

" We shan't starve," declared Rodney.

" Well, what can you do to keep from starving?" demanded his father. " You're not a producer. You never will be. You're just an idler. You couldn't earn five dollars a week. But you'll have a chance to try. You'll get out of my house to-night, or I'll have you thrown out."

"Now, father —"

"Not another word, sir, not another word," cried his father, and stamped out angrily into the hall.

Mary gave an involuntary sigh of relief: the scene was over. As for Rodney he turned to her with a weird glee.

"It's getting more like that play every minute," he chuckled.

"Oh, Rodney, Rodney, what have I done? I'm so, so sorry," snivelled Mary.

"You haven't done anything," Rodney answered. "Neither of us has. Father didn't seem to give us a chance to; he did it all —"

"Oh, Rodney, Rodney," Mary sighed again.

"You were bully the way you stuck up for me," said her lover. "When you said we'd starve together, I just choked all up."

"Please don't, Rodney," protested Mary, quite genuinely touched; and Rodney went on:

"Just because he's got a lot of money he seems to think there isn't any left for other people, but I'll show him. I may not have much at the start, but watch my finish—"

"What are you going to do?" she asked him excitedly.

"I'm going to work."

"You are — really?"

"Yes, indeed — Father couldn't make me do it, but you can. I'll work for you."

"Oh, you are splendid," Mary cried. "Shall you get a position?"

"I should say not! Work for some one else? No! I'm going in business for myself — for you. I'm going to show the stuff that's in me. Of course we can't get married till I've made good. Will you wait?"

"Yes, dear," said Mary shyly.

"You're a dandy," cried Rodney, moving nearer to her.

"What business are you going into?" she asked.

"I don't know yet," said Rodney. "I'm going upstairs to pack a suit case and think. Wait here for me. I'll be back in fifteen minutes," he sang out, grabbing her and kissing her hastily but heartily.

"Oh, oh — please —" Mary protested.

"Don't mind, Mary, I'll get you used to 'em," he called from the doorway.

She threw herself back on the Louis XV sofa, next the yellow typist's desk, and waited, in a sudden revery. The carved, wooden rim of the sofa back just fitted a chink in her coiffure comfortably: and she lapsed into that curious state of introspection that comes sometimes with bodily and mental relaxation. What did she think of herself for what she'd done this evening? Was she any better than an adventuress? Was she not cajoling a young man into proposing to her for the love of money? Would Rodney's father really reward her as he had promised to do? Strangely enough it would not have seemed so bad, she felt, if she didn't like Rodney. Well, if the old man didn't pay, let him keep his money: she shouldn't care. It was something to have won a love like Rodney's love for her. There was something very lovable about Rodney Martin —

In a moment Rodney himself bounded in again on her day dreams. There was the thud of a heavy kit bag dropped on the marble floor of the hall by the front door, and then he ran in to her impetuously, with his arms open.

"Mary, sweetheart!" he cried.

He held her away from him a moment to regard her face.

"The pater's upstairs dressing for dinner," he rattled on. "I shan't even say good-by to him. Serve him right. I'm going to take a stage down to the Harvard Club this very night. Can't afford cabs now."

"Rodney," whispered Mary conservatively, "you must work hard and be brave."

"And can't I do that for the sweetest sweetheart in the whole world?" he demanded rapturously, folding her again in his arms. He hugged her greedily to him, and she yielded to him a little despite herself. There was something fresh and clean about the boy, and certainly his kisses were not distasteful. The arms she felt around her were a man's arms and very strong . . .

In the end Rodney decided he would have a cab anyway, and so he and Mary left the house of the soap king in each other's company, without farewells. It was their last ride together, so to speak, and a very blissful one for the young lover. Rodney was going to take a room at the Harvard Club, but first they spun across the somber park to Mary's apartment, somewhere in the West 70's, and Rodney bade her a rapturous good-night, while the motor throbbed and the taximeter spun.

CHAPTER IV

THE BARGAIN

CHAPTER IV

THE BARGAIN

MARY fell asleep with the memory of Rodney Martin's kisses on her lips, and felt his arms around her in her dreams, but woke to disillusion in the morning. What had she been thinking of to coquette with this nice boy like that? Was she a bold, designing woman, she asked herself again? It was too ridiculous. It was all very well to call it an elaborate ruse on old Mr. Martin's part to scare his son to work. She was ashamed of the part she had performed in it; she would drop the whole thing now, and just claim her money. She dressed and ate her breakfast and went out in a very virtuous and shamefaced state of mind.

She half looked forward, as she clung to her strap in the subway train going downtown, to finding the old gentleman in a tantrum at the office because she had taken him at his word. The sooner she extricated herself from the fantastic plot the better, she decided. When Cyrus Martin met her at his office he would find a curious change in her. He would summon her into his private room, she supposed, ostensibly to take some letters, and look her over quizzically, and perhaps remark: "Well, what happened?" and all that sort of thing.

As a matter of fact he did do and say all this, and added, a bit peevishly:

"You left me in suspense all night. The boy's gone too, I suppose you know."

The gout had been so benefited by the explosion of yesterday that he had gone down to his office next morning, as Mary guessed he would, and the two met there on somewhat more impersonal terms than in the Fifth Avenue library. Very impersonal indeed Mary tried to make it seem to the wily magnate, and threw something unwonted and chilly into the manner with which she greeted him. There was no longer that pleasant little feeling of conspiracy between them that he had enjoyed yesterday afternoon. What ideas were running through his old head? Mary wondered, as she surveyed him with an outward calm that was quite complete. She thought she could guess. Was her money going to turn her head so soon, she could fancy him thinking, or rather was it the mere prospect of some money? For it had not been turned over to her quite yet. He hoped that she had truly won it just the same, and that Rodney's departure was not just a bluff, for he believed twenty-five hundred dollars must be something of a boost to a girl in her position, and his manœuver was at least one way of not letting her left hand know what his right hand did for her. He would take some credit to himself for the transaction, of course, like most other rich men, and would not mind if his generosity were uncovered, provided the discovery came about in such a way as to leave him unjostled in his pose of modesty before Miss Mary Grayson. He liked the girl. But what was the matter with the little minx this morning? She could read all this more or less plainly on his hardened but sometimes transparent countenance.

"Well," he began again presently, "do you think our scheme is going to work?"

"Yes," said Mary quietly, "I do."

"You really think you have got him to go to work?" he demanded eagerly.

"I have," said Mary.

"By George, that's great!" said Mr. Martin gleefully.

"Isn't it?" said Mary.

"You're sure he wasn't just talking?"

"No, he went upstairs to pack and go out and make a name for himself."

"You're a wise girl, Mary. Isn't it wonderful?"

"And you said I couldn't do it," said Mary coldly.

"I said I didn't think you could, but you have, and I owe you twenty-five hundred dollars."

"Oh, there's no hurry," said Mary, still quite coolly.

"Never put off till to-morrow the money you can get to-day," said the millionaire.

"Aren't you proud I've been so successful," said Mary presently.

"Proud! I'm so darned happy I'm making this check out for five thousand dollars."

"Oh, Mr. Martin," Mary cried, quite taken aback.

"It's worth fifty thousand dollars to me to have my boy really want to work, not just to do it to please me," said the old man, really moved beneath his gruff exterior. "What a difference an incentive makes."

"Doesn't it?" said Mary, smiling at her check.

"Especially if it's a girl," Martin went on; "and to think I begged and threatened Rodney for months, and then you plan this scheme, you rehearse me. Bing — you make him fall in love with you."

"Well, the idea, Mr. Martin," cried Mary. "The scheme was yours."

"Nonsense, my dear, it was yours. And is he really in love with you?"

"He thinks he is."

"But what about your marriage?"

"He said he wouldn't marry me till he'd made good — if I'd just wait."

Her employer looked at her a little anxiously.

"Do you think perhaps he may really love you?" he asked.

"Of course not," said Mary.

"It's the first time he's actually wanted to marry anybody," said his father.

"Oh, it's just that I've been very blue-eyed and baby-faced," said the secretary modestly.

"I guess you're right!" agreed Martin.

"Of course I am. Why, dear Mr. Martin, even for this," she said, pointing to her check, "I wouldn't give your son one real pang. He's too nice a boy. When I break our engagement he may feel a bit lonely, and be very sorry for himself for a few days, and give up women forever; but pretty soon some charming girl of his own position — of his own world, who needs to be petted and spoiled and protected, some limousine lady — will come along, and they'll live happily ever after."

"Nonsense," said Mr. Martin, "I don't agree with you at all. I begin to wish this marriage were going to be on the level."

"It wouldn't work out," Mary interrupted. "I'm a business woman. Marriage and the fire-side and leaning on some man are not for me. I've been independent too long. I couldn't stop my work for a man, and there can't be two heads in a family — two happy heads. Even if your son did love me — really love — I wouldn't marry him. Just now he's twenty-four, with an India rubber heart that is easy to stretch and easier to snap back. All men at twenty-four are like that."

"I suppose so," Mr. Martin commented reminiscently. "I remember when I was a young man, there was a girl — my heart was broken for a week — perhaps ten days — however, however —" Then, abruptly changing the subject, he inquired, "What's my son going to work at?"

"I don't know yet," Mary said truthfully.

"Do you think he'll make good?"

"He will if he keeps at it."

"Well, you'll keep him at it? Won't you?"

"That wasn't our agreement," said Mary, "I only undertook to get him to start to work."

"Hm —," went Mr. Martin, tapping the arm of his chair.

"Isn't that true?" demanded Mary quietly.

"Quite — quite," said Martin cannily; "I was just thinking we might make some agreement to have you keep him on the job."

"To keep him on the job?" echoed Mary faint-heartedly. Here was a new complication, if the soap king was proposing a second chapter in the deception. She had honestly meant to give the whole thing up; she truly did not want Rodney to get permanently interested in her. She had let him kiss her — the memory of his kisses still trembled on her lips — but she had done that for the boy's own good. Poor little secretary, pretty little Mary Grayson, what was she to think of things, how cleave her way through this tangle of motives that bound her heart and hands? She had let him kiss her, yes, but had it really been wrong in her? — Was it — bad? No, she found her whole soul protesting, it was not wrong or bad. It had been for the boy's own good, she told herself again. She hugged the thought greedily, tasting a portion of that joy of women in giving herself up to some man for his good. But she would not spoil his life; she had been firm as to that. And now here was old Mr. Martin coming back at her with this hateful power of money and trying to bribe her to go on. What should she do? —

Suddenly, by a complete change of venue, her

thoughts attacked the case from a different angle. She had been enough in the business world to know the power and use of money, and from a French grandfather she had inherited a streak of keen and honest thrift. Let the rich people look out for themselves: the poor had to. Curiosity, too, set in, and helped dictate her answer when she finally made it.

"Well," she said at last, enigmatically, "I'm a business woman."

Mr. Martin looked at her delightedly.

"What strikes you as fair?" he asked her.

"I'd rather the proposition came from you," rejoined Mary.

"What do you say to your present salary, and at the end of the year I will personally give you a check for twenty-five per cent. of what he has made?"

"That wouldn't interest me," said Mary.

"What's your proposition then?" asked Martin. "State your terms."

"My present salary doubled," said the business woman promptly.

"Um — that's pretty steep."

"You told me what I'd done already was worth fifty thousand dollars to you," retorted Mary.

"Merely a figure of speech, my dear," said

Martin. "Let's see, you're getting forty dollars a week, and —"

"Fifty dollars, and I want one hundred."

"Sounds like a hold up."

"Then let's drop it. This new contract was your idea, not mine. Good evening —"

With that she moved over to the door behind him, which she banged shut as if she had gone. She remained, however, in the room and watched him keenly.

"Hold on, hold on," Martin cried after her.

He turned and saw her, and then chuckled at her joke on him, as she laughed too.

"I was simply figuring," he explained; "tell you what I'll do. Seventy-five dollars a week and ten per cent. of what he makes."

"All right, I'll go you," said Mary.

"Good," said Mr. Martin.

"Will you just write me a note stating the facts and the consideration?" Mary pursued.

"Certainly."

He began to write, and as his pen moved across the paper Mary went on:

"As soon as you see Rodney, you'll have to discharge me. He may come in here to-day, thinking you're home."

"I will, violently. I'm a pretty good actor under your direction."

"You needn't make the note long," said Mary. "Just a memorandum."

"How's that?" he said, holding up a paper.

Mary read it, and remarked, "I think that covers it; — if you'll sign it."

"Didn't I sign it?" he asked in some confusion.

"No, and never put off till to-morrow what you can sign to-day," said Mary, smiling.

Martin signed it, and handed it to her with a hearty, "There you are!"

It had developed after all into a brisk and businesslike interview, and old Martin seemed quite pleased at the way he had put it through. He would be sorry to have her go, really, as she must if she was going to help Rodney in his money-making. It wasn't so easy to make money, as they both knew, and the boy would need all the help he could to keep him on the job.

As for Mary, she had discerned that Rodney would demand her services when she should be discharged — of course; and began to wonder how the next scene should be arranged. Mr. Martin was as good at making scenes as a typical stage father, he told her with a chuckle. He would watch over the boy a bit, of course, and play fairy godfather now and then, without showing his hand. The boy would need some capital, he rattled on. Let's see, how should he get it? Well, he could raise some money selling his aëroplane — silly thing it was, anyway; and his three cars. It would be a good thing to get rid of all that junk, anyway. In addition Rodney had perhaps a thousand in the bank, the remnants of the check his father had bestowed on him. Then there was old Uncle William Smith. Martin would arrange to have Smith advance some money to the boy if he were approached, as he would be, probably, in the guise of the oldest friend of the family.

He summed all this up to his confederate, Mary, and altogether things looked pretty good to the soap king, as he closed his desk, and stepped gingerly out of the office on his way home at three o'clock. He didn't have his car come all the way down town for him except on very stormy days; he considered it too soft and luxurious. But then he did not ride in the subway at the time of its greatest crush either. Mary could see him smiling benevolently as he glanced over the headlines in his *Evening Post,* and thought how cleverly he had managed. As for poor Mary herself she viewed the future with much less complacency, being less certain of her own mind. She was not sure that old Martin had not laid the train for more troubles than either of them was aware of at that moment.

CHAPTER V

THE RIVALS

CHAPTER V.

THE RIVALS

AFTER leaving Mary in West 70th Street, the night he had abandoned the paternal roof, Rodney, still in his taxicab, was whirled down, alone and in a perfect dream of happiness, to the Harvard Club, where he planned to spend his first night. If love's young dream meets with rude awakenings, the dream is glorious while it lasts. Rodney chatted awhile with a few of the fellows who dropped into the pleasant room, and even drank one mild high ball before he went to bed, but his head swam with a far more powerful stimulant than rye or Scotch. He listened to his companion's chatter in a mellow and golden mood, and finally went upstairs and turned in with a kindly feeling toward all the world. No one would have dreamed that he had just been cast out of his father's house, and faced work for the first time in his life.

He lay in his strange bed and reviewed the events of this hectic evening long before he closed his eyes in sleep, the memory of Mary's kisses making everything warm and rosy. Through it all he recalled his father's harsh words with curious insistence too. And how had he, Rodney, acted, he wondered, through it all, and what had Mary thought of him?

So far as his own inclinations had run there was no doubt in the boy's mind what he would do, he had said to himself decisively, when his father spoke. If this was a bluff on his father's part he would call it promptly. The next time the old man asked Johnson where "Mr. Rodney" was, "Mr. Rodney" would be out — gone, never to return.

He had skipped upstairs to his room, two steps at a time, and begun flinging things out of drawers and chiffoniers. What trunk should he take? That new Vuitton he had had made in Paris last summer, "before the war"? No, he could send for that later, and besides he didn't want to stay away from Mary any longer than he could help. He wouldn't take all his things just now: he would leave a good many behind, so that his father would be sorry if he ever came into his room again after his baby boy was gone. He would not take a trunk at all now, just his kit bag. Where was that kit bag? Johnson would know.

He started to ring for Johnson and then checked himself. He would not say anything to the servants yet. He didn't want them to be a party to this painful scene. He would leave them misinformed, and keep his father guessing a little while. He would go and get that kit bag himself. It was in the garret most likely.

He had sneaked up the narrow garret staircase, the boards creaking now and then beneath his tread, just as they used to do when he was a child. A flood of old, odd memories swept over him as the attic door opened. There was the old hobby horse, life size, that had been given him when he was a kid, its right flank badly moth eaten now, and one glass eye removed by time or the hard knocks of fate. Not far away was an eleemosynary portrait of his mother, which had never looked like her, and had not been tolerated in her lifetime, though now his father threatened intermittently to dig it out and bring it downstairs again. Under the eaves he spied his kit bag, covered with dust. He dragged at it, and a pile of magazines and odds and ends of books fell forward across his arms. One of them was a battered cash book or old diary, bound with a black and white back, and with many recipes written in a refined feminine hand on its blank pages. Rodney remembered this well; it was a real heirloom from the Earles, his mother's people, who had prided themselves on "setting a good table." Rodney sat down on his dusted kit bag and turned over the yellowing pages idly. Some of the recipes were in an even older hand than his mother's — his grandmother's, or his maiden aunts' probably — and now and then, in his mother's hand again, there would be a comment written in the margin — "Very choice," or "Extra good," or "Well worth trying." When the régime of the French chef had begun in the Martin kitchen this old volume had been banished to the attic, so it seemed, but Rodney remembered it well. The recipes for these tasty old dishes looked good just the same. Rodney decided to tuck the book in with his own things, a venial theft, and put it by some day for himself and Mary. They certainly did sound good. "Old Farrington meat pie," "Hannah Earle's gold and silver cake," "Susan Pitcher's Everlasting Fruit Cake." — Yes, he would take it. And here was a formula even for soap, and in his mother's hand, or his grandmother's — he could not be sure which — was the quaint marginal note: "The cheapest soap in the world: Unlucky for dirt." And so he had pitched the old book into the bag, stolen down the attic stairs again, and bounded, dusty kit bag and all, into the little waiting room where Mary sat —

Dear Mary!

And she had let him hug her — the first taste of the bliss to come. How sweet and wonderful she was . . .

When he woke in the morning he rubbed his eyes a moment in bewilderment at his unaccustomed surroundings. And immediately the memory of Mary Grayson swept over him again, fresh and undimmed. Somehow it was a surprise to him, but a gratification, too, to be just as much in love in the morning, before breakfast, as he had been the night before. He sang as he jumped beneath the shower bath across the hall, and bummed and sang as he dressed and went down to breakfast. He would call up Mary on the telephone before she got away to the office. And, by the way, he had an idea to tell her too. He was going to make soap, like his father. The old cook book had given him the idea. He left his coffee scarcely tasted and flew to a booth.

"Well, Mary," he shouted through the receiver, which smelt of cigarettes, "did you know I'd lost my job?"

"Yes," said Mary's voice at a distance. "I suppose I shall lose mine, too, if I don't give you up."

"We should be friends in need then," bawled Rodney at his end.

"Oh, Rodney, I'm so sorry," said Mary.

" Gout's an awful thing, isn't it? " shouted Rodney.

" Oh, Rodney! I'm afraid I've spoiled everything for you — your future."

" Nonsense, you've made my future. Without you I'd never have got the idea — the big idea."

" Idea for what? "

" The idea to make money out of — that's all you need — and, just think, I found it in an old book —"

" What idea — what book? "

" It's a cook book."

" What on earth —? "

" Well, you see when I was packing, I stumbled across an old family cook book. It fell open at a certain page — fate was on the job — it was a hunch —"

" But what is it? "

" It's an old family recipe for making cheap soap. It says it's the cheapest soap in the world. Cheaper even than the manufacturers make it. I'm going into the soap business."

" What? "

" Sure — father did — look at the money he made. Why shouldn't I? "

" You're joking —"

" I'm in dead earnest — I'm going to buck the trust —"

"But how can you?"

"I don't know, but I will. You see I'll have all the popular sympathy—independent young son of soap king fights father—don't buy from the trust."

"But is that very nice to your father?"

"Has he been very nice to me? It's great.—Down with monopoly.—Hurrah for the people—I've heard political speeches like that—Hurrah for the people's soap;—that isn't a bad name either—the People's Soap."

"But you haven't any capital."

"I never thought of that," Rodney answered dejectedly.

"You'd need a lot of money, too."

"Well," Rodney said, "well—I'll just have to get it, that's all, and you'll be my secretary. Of course, till I'd made big money I shouldn't ordinarily have thought of taking you away from father—"

"Rodney, you must stop talking, or you'll go stony broke with this long call," yelled Mary.

"Well, when can I see you again?" Rodney persisted.

"I shall be at the offiee till three," said Mary.

"I'll drop in. Father may be home with the gout," Rodney answered.

Rodney hung up the receiver and turned away

reluctantly. Mary's voice — wasn't it the most wonderful voice in the world? If Mary would come and work with him, then everything would be different. How could she go on with the old man after the way he'd treated his son? If she came with him, Rodney, he should have her near him, see her every day, hear her voice. He didn't care whether he succeeded or not; but then he would succeed, with the inspiration of his love for her to spur him on.

Of course the old man was throwing a kind of bluff, thought Rodney; he wouldn't really allow his son to land in the workhouse, or starve to death. But the old man would carry things through with a high hand, too, and in the end it would come to the same net result in discomfort and the long wait for Mary. He must work very, very hard: — oh, so hard. He took out a cigarette, and lit it, finding a quiet seat near the 44th Street window to sit down and think things over. There was no use getting excited: on the contrary there was every reason to keep cool. He armed himself with a newspaper, so that he could occasionally hold it up and ward off unwelcome chatterers who might disturb his train of thought. The armament was not modern enough, however, to repel the attack of the alert young man who presently came and peered over the top of his *Sun*.

"Well, Ambrose Peale," said Rodney, looking up.

"That's me absolutely," said Mr. Peale. "The same, at your service. So you remember me, eh?"

The sight of Peale's keen and eager face took Rodney back two years at a jump. The two boys had met one night in the lobby of a Boston theater, under circumstances that would have been peculiar and unconventional a hundred miles from a college town. The occasion had been an egg-fight, not between Rodney and Ambrose Peale, but between the audience and the stage. It had been a very lively and savory affair indeed, quite efficiently carried through by the college students scattered out in front; what might, in fact, have been called an old comedy revival, since the good old days of egg-throwing, when audiences had been wont to demonstrate their disfavor by hurling well chosen but badly preserved missiles and projectiles across the foot-lights, had till then, and for many years, enjoyed disuse in Boston, like stage soliloquies in the modern drama. It had been a college play, and had seemed to the student observers of it so lacking in verisimilitude that they had set up a counter demonstration in front, to show probably what real college life was like. Rodney had not thrown any eggs himself, because he had forgotten to bring any with him, a circumstance which was the saving of him, for it had been noted by Peale, the manager of the piece, and brought him to the rescue. Peale had been very decent to him, and kept him out of jail, thereby saving him numerous cuts, unlike the other fellows who had been duly haled before the Dean and suspended, besides figuring salaciously in the headlines of the Boston papers. Some of the more luckless ones even were featured under their own names. Altogether it was one of those specially illuminated moments of a fellow's life from which the impressions are long retained. Of course he remembered Ambrose Peale.

Mr. Peale vowed he had been looking for Rodney for a week, but with no success.

"Very mysterious about you up on the Avenue yesterday," he said. "What's up?"

"Just a little family row," said Rodney. "What's your line now?"

"Well, I'm still in the show business," said Peale. "Ever see the 'Belle of Broadway'? Great show, great girls, great cast."

"Oh, are you an actor?" asked Rodney carelessly.

"An actor? I should say not," said Peale scornfully. "I'm a press agent."

"Oh! I see," said Rodney.

"But say," rattled Peale; "be sure to catch that show. It may leave town soon — out of town bookings, you know — but remember the name, 'Belle of Broadway.'"

"I've heard of it," said Rodney.

"Well, if you'll excuse me, I've been looking for you to talk business with you. Shall I blaze away?" asked Peale.

"Business? Surely, surely," rejoined Rodney, with an inward wink. "I'm a business man now. Blaze away, as you say."

Ambrose Peale was one of those young Americans for whom a special series of new words has been minted. He was a hustler and he certainly was breezy; he was a live wire and he had the gift of the gab. He was not born yesterday and he would never really grow old. He turned up everywhere, like a bad penny, which nevertheless rang true. He had even taken a special course at Harvard for a time — to get next to "that college stuff," he had explained, and he occupied the seat next to the soap king's son at the club now in his own divine right.

"Well, well," said Peale, reminiscently, "I could see at once you weren't an egg thrower, but I wouldn't have blamed you anyhow. It was a rotten show."

"Like the eggs?" put in Rodney, smiling.

"Absolutely," said Peale. "Now I'm not much on handing myself flowers across the footlights, but do you happen to remember what I did for you?"

"You fixed things up with the chief of police," said Rodney, "and kept me from being expelled."

"By George, you do remember," Peale echoed. "And you said any time you could do anything for me —"

"That's still true," said Rodney.

"You're immense, son. Now, it's this way — Have a chair — Between you and me 'The Belle of Broadway' is an awful thing. Business gone to pot — something's got to be done. Some great stuff pulled off to give it a boost and that's where you come in. That's my business with you."

"With me?" said Rodney.

"You've got an aëroplane, haven't you?" inquired Peale plaintively.

"Yes — but —" began Rodney. "Let's go upstairs then," he added as an afterthought.

He knew Peale of old, and that if he got started there was nothing that could hush his voice for other members. In the big room in the 44th Street side upstairs they would be unmolested at this hour of the morning. In a few days Rodney too would be among the army to whom club rooms at this hour were unfamiliar haunts. Peale followed him in a docile manner. Time and place were no objects to Ambrose Peale. He just talked straight ahead in all places and seasons. There was something hypnotic and persuasive about him when he got started. He did not bother with rhetorical flourishes, or putting " expression " into his speeches, but just hit out keenly at his mark.

" Then everything's all right," said Peale eagerly. " Now you abduct the leading lady — Julie Clark — to-morrow night, in your aëroplane — elope with her."

" What? "

" Sure! Some stunt, too. Never been done. Julia's all for it. She's game for any press gag —"

" But I couldn't do such a thing as that," protested Rodney.

" Certainly you can," said Peale. " I'm telling you Julia'll stand for it — a bird of a story.— Why — you're up in the air with the leading lady. —The next night standing room only to catch a look at the girl you're stuck on.— I can see the headlines now:— Soap King's Son Takes New Star Among the Stars with Flashlights —"

" But it's out of the question," said Rodney.

" What's the matter with it? " demanded Peale.

" I wouldn't do it — that's all."

" Gee, that's tough on me," sighed Peale.

"I'm not backing down from helping you," said Rodney, "but there's some one who might object."

"A girl?" asked Peale acutely.

Rodney nodded.

"I guess it's cold," Peale concluded; "girls are funny about their beaux doing a little innocent thing like eloping with some other girl."

"Why don't you try somebody else?" suggested Rodney.

"I have! You were my last card. Well, I'm fired!" said Peale with an air of finality.

It was a stunt that would have kept things going, he protested; but now, well, the show was so bad that people wouldn't even go to see it on a pass. They would have to close Saturday, and as for Ambrose Peale, he was out. Rodney did not believe that an obvious faked up lie like that would have done any good, he said; he'd feel very uncomfortable at not being able to oblige an old friend, otherwise.

"I know it's advertising," he said, "but —"

"You bet it's advertising," began Peale, warming up. "What made Anna Held? — Milk baths. — What made Gaby Deslys? — A dago king."

"But that sort of advertising can't be of real value," said Rodney, negligently.

"Oh, you're one of those wise guys who don't believe in advertising, are you?" said Peale, expostulating and expounding. "Now don't get me talking advertising. That's where I live, where I have my town house and country estate, my yacht and motors.— That's my home. Maybe you think love is important. Piffle! Advertising, my boy; the power of suggestion, the psychology of print. Say a thing often enough — hard enough — and the other chap'll not only believe you, he'll think it's his own idea; and he'll fight for it.— Some old gink, a professor of psychology, showed forty Vassar girls, the other day, two samples of satin, one blue, one pink same grade — same value — same artistic worth. One he described as a delicate warm old rose — the other he called a faded blue. He asked them to choose their favorite. Girls picked the old rose. Why? Because they'd been told it was warm and delicate — no faded blue for theirs. What did it? Power of suggestion — advertising."

Rodney listened amazed and amused. Peale was off and away now at a rapid clip.

"You seem to know something about it," Rodney said aloud.

"I not only seem to — I do," Peale agreed. "You heard me say a few minutes ago to that fellow downstairs that 'The Belle of Broadway' was the biggest hit in town. Ask him to go to the theater, give him his choice, and I'll bet you four dollars to a fried egg he picks the Belle of Broadway.—Advertising!"

"I don't believe it," Rodney protested.

"Well, try it.—And say, what makes you go to the theater yourself? I'll tell you—it's what you've read about the play, or what some fellow's told you."

"Why, I suppose that's true," said Rodney, beginning to be convinced a little.

"And what he tells you some other guy has told him. Ninety-seven per cent. of the public believe what they're told, and what they're told is what the other chap's been told; and the fellow who told him read it somewhere. When you see a thing in print about something you don't really know anything about, you come pretty near believing it. And all the advertiser has to do is to tell you right and you'll fall—"

"But I never read advertisements," said Rodney.

"Oh, you don't eh? If I say fifty-seven varieties you know it means pickles. I guess you've got some idea that 'His Master's Voice' advertises a phonograph. You're on to what soap 'It floats' refers to. There's a Reason—Uneeda—All the News That's Fit to Print—

Quaker Oats — Children Cry for It — Grape Nuts — Peruna — The Road of Anthracite — Spearmint — Pierce-Arrow — Kodak — Mumm's — Gold Dust Twins — He Won't Be Happy Till He Gets It — Bull Durham — Pianola — Cuticura — Clysmic — Steinway — Coca Cola — The Watch That Made the Dollar Famous.— I suppose you don't know what any of them mean."

"Why, I know what they all mean," said Rodney much amused.

"You bet you do.— Say what kind of garters do you wear?"

"Why, let me see — Boston," said Rodney.

"Exactly," said Peale. "What do you know about 'em? Nothing. Are they any better than any other garter? You don't know — I don't know, but all my life every magazine I've ever looked into has had a picture of a man's leg with a certain kind of garter on it — Boston. So when I go into a store to buy a pair of garters I just naturally say, Boston, so do you. What do you know about Mennen's Talcum Powder? Nothing, except that it has the picture of the homeliest man in the world on the box, and it's so impressed your imagination you just mechanically order Mennen's. If I say to you E. & W. you don't think it's a corset, do you? If I say C. B. you don't think it's a collar. And what about the well known and justly famous B. V. D.'s? You don't read advertisements? Rot!"

"But—" said Rodney.

"No 'but' about it," answered Peale. "Advertising's responsible for everything. When Bryan advertised the Grape Juice Highball, do you know that its sale went up six hundred and fifty-two gallons a day?"

"You don't really mean it?"

"I do."

"But six hundred and fifty-two gallons. How do you know it was six hundred and fifty-two?" asked Rodney.

"I'll let you into a little secret," confided Peale. "I don't know a damned thing about grape juice—and as long as my health and strength keep up, I hope I never shall—but if I said I'd read in a newspaper that the sale had gone up six hundred and fifty-two gallons you wouldn't have doubted it, would you?"

"No, I suppose I shouldn't," Rodney agreed.

"And you'd have told somebody else, and he'd have believed you too," went on Peale. "The other day at Atlantic City one of the Show girls asked me how much it cost to light Young's Pier. I told her six hundred and forty-seven dollars a night. The next day three girls wanted to know if I knew the amazing fact that it cost six hundred and forty-seven dollars to light Young's Pier. I said I did."

"But does it cost that?" inquired Rodney.

"How do I know?" said Peale. "But don't you see they believed what they were told? So do you — so do I — so do all the other dubs. Say do you drink much?"

"No," said Rodney, thinking of Mary.

"Can you tell the difference between a vintage wine and last year's champagne?" demanded Peale. "Sure you can — it costs more. Son, the world is full of bunk. Ninety-seven per cent. of the people are sheep and you can get 'em all by advertising."

"You are gradually making me come to the conclusion that you believe in publicity," said Rodney politely.

"Believe in it! It's my life," cried Peale. "What kind of eggs do you eat?"

"Why hen's eggs — of course," Rodney laughed.

"Did you ever eat a duck egg?" asked Peale.

"Why, no," said Rodney. "At any rate, not often."

"Do you know anything against the duck?"

"No."

"Exactly. When a duck lays an egg it's a damn fool and keeps quiet about it, but when a hen does — my boy: Cluck — cluck, all over the place. Advertising. So you eat hen's eggs."

"You're beginning to convince me," laughed Rodney.

"That's advertising too," said Peale. "Say, are you for Roosevelt or against him?"

"I'm for him strong," said Rodney.

"I'm against him," said Peale. "I read one paper, you read another. I think he's a fakir, you think he's a great man. But do either of us really know anything about him except what we've read? Have you ever met Roosevelt or talked to him or known anybody who did know him? I haven't, but the point is, whatever we may think, good or bad, we've heard a lot about him, because he's the best advertiser in the world. And that, my son, is the whole secret of it. Get 'em talking about you. Get 'em praising if you can, or get 'em cussing, but for the love of Heaven don't let 'em be quiet. Mention your name. Have 'em argue about you. Boost or knock. Be a hero or a villain, but don't be a dub. Why, give me a little money and a few pages of advertising, and I can sell you shares in the Atlantic Ocean."

Rodney was beginning to get excited with all this advertising talk, and an idea began to shape itself in the back of his head.

"You really believe that with proper advertising, you could build up a great business?" he asked.

"Believe! Look around you. Everything's doing it," declared Peale.

"And you are out of a job?" went on Rodney.

"Unless you do the aero-elopement, yes," said Peale.

"Then you're out of it. Do you want to work for me?"

"Sure."

"When can you begin?"

"Now."

"What's your salary?" asked Rodney, the new business man.

"I've been getting sixty dollars, but I'm worth seventy-five," said Peale quickly.

"I'll give you a hundred," Rodney told him.

"What's your business — counterfeiting?" asked Peale skeptically.

"No, it's —" began Rodney.

"Don't tell me," Peale interrupted. "As long as it don't send me to State's prison or the chair, it's all right. Could I have about twenty-five dollars advance on salary now?"

"Is that customary?" inquired Rodney.

"It is with me," declared Peale.

"Oh, all right," said Rodney, handing him the money.

"Just as an evidence of good faith," Peale explained, counting the crisp bills. "Well, now, I'm working for you. What business are you in?" he began again.

"The soap business," said Rodney boldly.

"Nice clean business. With father?" asked Peale, grinning.

"Against him," explained Rodney.

"Oh," said Peale.

Rodney reminded him that he and his father had had a quarrel, and Peale agreed very sympathetically that fathers were very unreasonable these days.

"I'm going to fight the soap trust," said Rodney.

"Well, you've picked out a nice refined job. How long have you been at it?" asked Peale.

"Twenty minutes."

"How's it going?"

"Fine, since I got an idea from you."

"They grow all over me — help yourself," said Peale.

"I'm going to get a factory, and advertise like the very dickens," said Rodney. "Soap King's son fights father. And licks him too — by George."

"Wait a minute, wait a minute," Peale commented. "Do you know why your father is the soap king?"

"I suppose because he controls all the soap business in the country, except Ivory," said Rodney.

"Exactly; and the way he keeps control of it is by buying out all his live competitors. And now here's a blue ribbon champion of the world scheme. Why don't we make good and sell out to father?"

"No, I don't care to do that — I want to make good myself," said Rodney.

"Well, if father is forced to buy you out, isn't that enough? What do you want?" asked Peale.

"I've got to be a success on my own — I've got to show father, and — Miss Grayson," explained Rodney.

The name of Mary gave him courage to say this, and mean it too. His father may not have turned him out in good earnest, but Rodney began to hope he had; began to long for the time when he could show his mettle. He must show Mary as well as his father; and so he had no difficulty now in talking up to Peale. He went on now to explain:

"You see father says I can't earn five dollars a week."

"He isn't right, is he?" queried Peale anxiously.

"No, sir, you'll see," Rodney answered proudly.

"I hope so," said Peale drily. "At that, it's a pretty tough job selling soap if father's against us."

"I suppose it is," Rodney agreed.

"I'll tell you. Why not make such a hit he'll just have to back you?"

"That sounds good. We'll do it," said Rodney.

"Stick to me, kid, and you'll wear rubies," chanted Peale with a little swagger.

"Now that's settled. We're going to lick father," said Rodney.

"Yes, that's settled. What do I do?" asked Peale.

"You write the ads that make us."

"It's my chance," cried Peale enthusiastically. "Just think! I'll never have to see 'The Belle of Broadway' again. I'll write ads, I'll conduct a campaign that'll keep your father awake, and in three months at the most he'll be begging for a chance to back us."

At that moment, with the vision of Mary floating before his eyes, Rodney felt that the worst of fate was already conquered. It was Ambrose Peale who brought him down to soap and actuality. What was the name of the soap, this enterprising agent wanted to know. What was there about it that made it different from any other soap? What could there be about one soap that was different from another soap? Where did the idea come from?

When poor Rodney trotted out the story of the cook book, Peale wanted to know if he was "kidding him," but grew less skeptical when he heard all there was to hear about the cheapest soap in the world. It was a good line, he said, the cheapest soap. How could they use it? he inquired, pausing and thinking deeply, while Rodney was lost in business meditation too.

Suddenly Rodney called out:

"Peale, I've got an entirely different idea."

"Well, don't be selfish. Share it with me," said his partner.

"Why do the people jam the cabarets where they only serve champagne," began Rodney excitedly. "Why do they crowd the restaurants where they put up a rope to keep you out? Why do they sit in the sixteenth row in the orchestra when they could have the third row in the balcony? Why do they buy imported clothes? Why do they ride in French automobiles? Because they're better? No, because they're expensive; because they cost more money. So all the sheep think they ought to be better. My boy — listen — 'the most expensive soap in the world'!"

"My boy, I could kiss you," cried Peale delightedly. "A pupil after my own heart — fifty cents a cake," cried Peale.

"A dollar, and we'll make it a warm delicate old rose," sang Rodney.

"Each cake in a separate box, with a paper rose on the lid," said Peale. "But what shall we call it?"

"Old rose," suggested Rodney, after a moment.

"Rotten — doesn't mean anything," rejected Peale.

"Let's think," said Rodney.

"I am thinking. I never stop," said Peale.

"The soap that made Pittsburg clean," said Rodney.

"Too long, and no good anyway — because Pittsburg isn't clean. You need something catchy."

"I had an idea a while ago," said Rodney; "the People's Soap."

"Not if you're going to catch the rich boobs," said Peale.

"That's true," assented Rodney.

"We need something that's universally appealing. What is it?" began Peale.

"Love," said Rodney, his thoughts flying up town where he had seen Mary last.

"Slush," said Peale.

"I am thinking. I never stop," said Peale.

"Money," suggested Rodney, still thinking of Mary.

"No," cried Peale suddenly, "I've got it — Superstition — Everybody's superstitious."

"Rot — I'm not," argued Rodney.

"No, of course you're not," said Peale. "I say, there's a bit of luck for us right at the start — a pin with the head toward you."

Rodney stooped to pick it up.

"See, you were going to pick it up," chuckled Peale. "Everybody is superstitious. Oh, they say they're not, just as you did, but did you ever meet a guy who, if he didn't mind walking under a ladder, didn't hate to spill salt? Or else he wanted to see the moon over his right shoulder, or he picked up pins, or carried a lucky coin, or wouldn't do things on Friday? Why, the whole world's superstitious. Get something on that, and you hit everybody. I got eighty-six horseshoes home myself. I never saw a gink that would sit thirteen at table. We're all crazy."

They paused and thought again.

Could they? No. Suppose they did — What? No. They paused and thought again.

Then suddenly Rodney remembered the legend in the old cook book, and cried out:

"Wait, wait! Listen! Listen close. The 13 Soap. Unlucky for Dirt."

"Son," said Peale, coming over and kissing Rodney chastely on the brow, "it's all over. The old man'll be on his knees in a month."

"We open the office Monday," Rodney sang out.

"Where's the office?" Peale inquired.

"Let's get one," said Rodney.

"With furniture and everything," said Peale; "and say — you'd better call up your tailor and order a couple of business suits."

After this manner began the business of the great 13 Soap Company, which was to bring the Soap King Cyrus Martin to his knees and make Rodney a rich man in his own right so he could marry Mary Grayson.

CHAPTER VI

CHASING CAPITAL

CHAPTER VI

CHASING CAPITAL

WITH the dithyrambics of the rediscovered Ambrose Peale sounding in his ears the boy was thinking of Mary too all the time. She was the best girl in the world, Mary, his sweetheart, his motive power, his guiding force. Her name had been a long-held, dominant note, to use a musical simile, to which Peale's advertising talk had been the chromatic variations. The point came when Mary must be taken into the theme too. He was to see her again at his father's offiee, and the joyful hour was coming round. Rodney interrupted the irrepressible agent at last by explaining things to him, and inviting him to come along down town.

"We can talk in the subway," he apologized.

"Sure. I can talk anywhere," said Peale.

Surcharged with their new enthusiasm, they went out finally and over to the Grand Central subway station, Peale still talking. A drizzling rain had begun to fall, and gave promise of quite a downpour later, but nothing could put out the flying sparks of Peale's enthusiasm.

Rodney, when they had arrived safely at his father's office, first assuring himself of his father's being securely enclosed in his inner room — it had been a disappointment to find him down town at all to-day — was rewarded by a sight of Mary. He flew to her side and spoke to her, looking deep into her eyes to see if her love was still there. The examination made him oblivious of anything and everybody till finally he heard a loud and fairly well executed cough behind him from Ambrose.

He turned and introduced them.

"Pleased to meet you. Excuse my glove," said Peale, shaking hands with her. Then in an aside to Rodney, he added: "By the way, is this the dame? Ask her to go to the theater, just to prove what I say. See for yourself."

He turned his back ostentatiously.

"Oh, Mary, to celebrate, let's go to the theater to-morrow night," said Rodney. "Shall we?"

"I'd love to," answered Mary.

"What do you want to see?" he asked.

"I hear 'The Belle of Broadway' is very good," she answered.

Peale yawned and stretched out his arms complacently, remarking to Rodney, "I guess I don't know about advertising, eh? My last official act is giving you a box for to-morrow night." And he wrote out a pass for them.

"Are you with that play?" asked Mary politely.

"I am," said Peale, handing her the pass: "I was."

"But isn't it an imposition?" asked Mary.

"Not on us, it isn't," said Peale promptly.

"Thank you," said Mary; then turning to Rodney she added:

"I didn't mean to bother you, but I'm so interested, I thought regarding Mr. Peale's business,— I'd like to hear —"

"It's all settled, Mary," Rodney began. "Mr. Peale, my general manager. Mr. Peale, my secretary. Mary, here it is. The 13 Soap, Unlucky for Dirt. The most expensive soap in the world."

"Why, that's perfectly wonderful," said Mary genuinely, looking at Peale. "Who thought of it?"

"I did," said Rodney proudly.

"You did really? Why, you're splendid," applauded Mary.

"Youth, brains, efficiency — that's our motto," chanted Peale.

"We'll make a hundred thousand dollars the first year — sure," put in Rodney.

"And ten per cent. of that is —" began Mary reflectively.

"What?" asked Rodney mystified.

"Oh, nothing — nothing; — I was just figuring," corrected Mary.

"We're going to make our soap famous by advertising and then force father to back us," continued Rodney, full of his subject.

"That sounds awfully nice," said Mary, "and at the start you won't need much capital."

"Capital?" repeated Rodney, as if the word were new to him.

"With fifty thousand dollars I can make the Great American people have hysterics over 13 Soap," said Peale.

"Fifty thousand dollars," repeated Rodney, sitting down flat; "and I haven't got but one thousand to my name."

"But can't you raise it?" queried Peale anxiously.

But how, thought Rodney cudgelling his brains hard. Fifty thousand already looked very large to this rich man's son. He stared at Peale, who, however, returned him no encouragement.

"Don't ask me," he protested. "Raising money is the only thing I never got onto. The only way I know to make a lot of money quick is to teach tango dancing."

"Well, Peale, you're fired then," said Rodney; "you've lost your job. Give me back that twenty-five dollars."

"Well, it was a nice job while it lasted," said Peale pathetically. "Good-by," he added, apostrophizing the greenbacks as he handed them to Rodney; "you're the only thing I've ever loved."

It was Mary who asked if they could not possibly do with less, and then they began to take account of possibilities. Of course they could, Rodney said, and appealed to Ambrose, the skeptical one, where money was concerned. Not and do it right, this gentleman averred. There was no use wasting money piking when you advertised: you must splurge, my lad, splurge. But Rodney, in his neophytic enthusiasm, persisted in thinking the thousand dollars he had in the bank could be put to some use anyway. And Mary was inclined to support him. Then the aeroplane was worth four thousand; it cost eight thousand and might bring two. The motors ought to bring another four with any kind of luck. That would make seven. Surely that was something. Peale allowed it was a sum not to be spoken of venomously, but in advertising it might just about last a week. To Rodney's surprise Mary spoke up presently and announced that she might be able to get hold of five thousand.

"I have — I know a man, that might put in that much," she said hestitatingly.

Rodney looked at her curiously.

"Why, Mary, you're fine," he said proudly. "And that would make twelve."

Even Peale was encouraged by this total.

"Does your father advertise much?" he asked Rodney suddenly.

Rodney didn't think so, and turned to Mary, who described the elder Martin as very conservative, and not a great believer in advertising and publicity.

"Why, the poor old nut," said Peale; "he's licked now, and I'll tell you why. We can advertise just for your father's benefit alone."

"But I don't quite understand your plan," said Mary, turning to the press man curiously.

"Why, plaster the neighborhood of his house with advertisements on all the fences," said Peale, turning loose again on this pet topic; "do the same around his office, so that every time he goes out or comes in he'll see 13 Soap. We can advertise only in the newspapers he reads — we'd send him circulars every day. I could make a splurge just for him that would look like we were giving up ten thousand dollars a day. Within a month he'd think that 13 Soap was the only soap in the wide, wide world."

"How much would it take?" asked Rodney.

"Five thousand a week," said Peale, figuring rapidly.

"And you could land him in a month?" asked Rodney.

"My boy! Do you doubt me?"

"And we've got one thousand all cash and eleven thousand in prospects. Go ahead," said Rodney emphatically.

"You mean I'm hired again?" inquired Peale, delighted.

"Of course, you are."

"Gimme back that twenty-five dollars."

Rodney handed it back, and Peale pocketed it confidently, informing him that the best thing he, Rodney, had ever done had been to engage Ambrose Peale, and that with Rodney's money and his, Ambrose Peale's, ideas, they would all be millionaires. Rodney and Mary certainly hoped so, and Rodney at least looked meaningly at his lady love as the vision of his own riches floated round him.

They had been all this time in the outer office, which on account of the rain had been invaded by few callers that day, though Mary had been interrupted by the telephone too often to please her jealous lover. It was a more or less typical waiting-room. The walls were done in a kind of mahogany paneling, with pictures hung above them representing the various "works" in which the company had lived. There was also a very stiff likeness of Rodney's uncle, who had been a partner in the business at the time of his death. The looks of this uncle had always affected Rodney very peculiarly until to-day, he disliked his whiskered physiognomy so intensely; but to-day even the avuncular whiskers seemed mellow and golden.

From time to time an under-secretary or sub-typewriter stuck her head through the door and announced some one. This young person opened the door now suddenly and announced with mingled glee and curiosity:

"The Countess de Bowreen!"

Money, when you are chasing it up in the form of capital, is a real will o' the wisp. Now you see it within your grasp, and again your gaze is quite blank. None of the three conspirators in the room realized what was to come of the French and titled lady's interruption, and only looked upon her as an inconvenient bore, to be disposed of as best could be.

"Oh, that dreadful woman again," sighed Mary.

The Countess entered and came over to Rodney at once, speaking to him in French:

"Vousêtes Monsieur Martin?" she cooed.

Rodney nodded.

"Ah, cher Monsieur Martin — je suis enchantée de vous voir."

"The dame's looney," said Peale in an aside to Mary.

"No — she's French," said Mary.

"Same thing," said Peale.

"What's all this anyhow?" Rodney inquired, half vexed.

"She wanted to see your father, and she doesn't speak English," said Mary. "I saw her up at the house."

"Well, let her talk to me," Rodney announced, remembering that he had taken a course in elementary French at Harvard.

"Say, can you speak French?" asked Peale, surprised and impressed by his new partner's aecomplishments.

"Not very well, but I can understand it," said Rodney. Then going over to the Countess, he said blankly in English: "Fire ahead."

"Eh?" said the Countess.

"Let me see — oh, yes — Parlez," stuttered Rodney.

"Ah, mon Dieu — enfin — vous comprenez Français?" began the Countess delightedly.

"Oui," said Rodney.

"You're immense, kid," put in Peale.

The one French word was enough to start up the Countess at her best gait.

"Je suis Madame la Comtesse de Beaurien — je desire parler à Monsieur Martin apropos des affaires du savon. Je voudrais obtenir l'agence du savon Martin pour la France," she rattled off in one breath.

"Wait a minute — wait a minute," said Rodney.

"What did she say?" asked Mary.

"She's a speedy spieler all right," said Peale.

"Would you mind saying that over, and say it slow?" asked Rodney of the Countess.

"Eh?" said that lady again.

"Oh — Repetez ça s'il vous plait — lentement," stumbled Rodney.

"Je suis Madame la Comtesse de Beaurien — Je desire obtenir l'agence du savon Martin pour la France — Je peux donner cinquante mille francs pour cette agence."

"Oui," said Rodney, quite pleased with himself; upon which the Countess was off again:

"Et enfin — voulez-vous arranger cette affaire pour moi? J'ai beaucoup de references. Je suis riche; je suis bien connue à Paris."

"Wait a minute — wait a minute," protested

Rodney. Then turning to Peale he interpreted plausibly:

"She wants the agency for father's soap for France, and is willing to pay fifty thousand francs for the concession."

"How much is that in real money?" asked Peale quickly.

"Ten thousand dollars," said Rodney.

"Had I better tell your father?" asked Mary. But Rodney had an inspiration:

"No, no, why not keep father out of this. We'll sell her the agency for the 13 Soap; that'd be another ten thousand for us. Peale, she's a gift from the gods."

"Go to it," said Peale, elated.

"But how can you sell her your agency?" objected the prudent Mary.

"I don't know; how can I?" wondered Rodney.

"A pipe — Ask her if she's superstitious?" put in Peale.

"Oh, if I only really knew how to talk French," said Rodney plaintively; then attempting bravely, he added:

"Madame — etes-vous superstitieuse?"

"Eh?" said the Countess.

"She don't get you?" inquired Peale anxiously.

"No."

But Ambrose Peale was a man of resource. He went over and took the Countess's parasol and started to raise it, whereupon with a cry of protest she stopped him, looking very ruffled and upset.

"She's superstitious all right," said Peale. "It ought to be a pipe to get her."

Then Rodney tried again.

"Listen," he said; "je suis le fils de Museer Martin — vous savez?"

"Oui, oui —" said the Countess delightedly.

"Nous manufacturons un nouveau savon," said Rodney. "Savon Treize," and he held up his fingers to indicate thirteen.

"Oui, oui," ejaculated the Countess.

Ambrose Peale was more and more impressed.

"Gee, a college education is certainly great; she understands every word you say," he exclaimed enthusiastically.

"Savon Treize — pas — bon pour — what the deuce is dirt — oh yes — sal — pas bon pour sal," continued Rodney.

"Savon Treize — pas bon pour sal. C'est bien — c'est bien," repeated the Countess eagerly.

"She likes it — she likes it," shouted Peale in great glee.

"Je start un nouveau compagnie — la tres grande compagnie de l'universe. Je suis le president."

"He took the Countess's parasol and started to raise it."

"Je suis le advertising agent," chipped in Peale.

"I'm the whole thing, see?" Rodney went on; "and if we can do business with you for the French agency we should be glad to."

The Countess, upon this harangue, still shrugged her shoulders as if mystified, though there was a look in her eyes that made Mary, who had seen her before, think she was not completely without an idea of what Rodney was driving at.

"If only Marie were here to interpret for us," sighed Mary.

The three partners looked at each other helplessly. They felt as if there were something hovering round that ought not to be allowed to get away, and yet it still eluded them.

"I suppose Marie's the French maid," said Peale. "Doesn't she ever come to the office? It might pay us to send up for her. Get a taxi. Buy one, to get ten thousand dollars back on it."

But as luck would have it Marie herself burst through the door at this moment, shrieking violently at the under-secretary in her native gibberish. She was another gift from heaven, said Rodney. It was the work of a few minutes to introduce the two compatriots and turn them loose on each other. They both talked at once, and as if they were having a race to see which could talk the louder and the faster, while Mary, Peale and Rodney stood by impressed and bewildered. They had not an idea why Marie had appeared at the office, but just accepted her as part of their good luck. Rodney bundled the two of them into a side room, so the rest could hear themselves think, he said. Then he sent Mary and Peale after them, Mary, on second thoughts, to translate Peale's slang, and Marie to put it into French. Left alone in the waiting-room he looked toward the door through which they had disappeared and almost prayed.

Without Mary, and with the possibility of seeing his father again any moment he felt very uncomfortable. He should hate to be discovered there in his father's offices: it would be almost as bad as having stayed on at his father's house after being turned out for good. He had left that home precipitately, and certainly did not mean to return unless he could not help it. He still had too much pride for that.

Suddenly a door opened and he started guiltily, but his fears turned to hope when he saw Mr. William Smith coming in. Old Uncle William Smith, one of the oldest friends of the family, had been one of the capital possibilities he had had in mind.

Mr. Smith was not really an uncle, but only bore that title by way of courtesy. Rodney's mother and Mrs. Smith had been at school together, and their children, in the tender years when the real and the pretended are not clear to them in the matter of uncles, had always looked upon their elders as related. Uncle William Smith, when Rodney was a boy, used to make a great show of looking through all his pockets to see if he had a nickel in them for him. Would he find anything now? He would tackle Uncle William for ten thousand dollars. Would he fall? Well, he could try.

Peale stuck his head through the door at this moment to catch Rodney's eye and execute a large and on the whole encouraging wink apropos of the French interview. Rodney gave another wink to Peale that said volumes about Mr. Smith, who indeed looked substantial and moneyfied enough to mean something to Peale without this commentary.

"That's all now, Mr. Peale," said Rodney, raising his voice.

"Yes, sir, I understand," said Peale, winking again. "He takes fifty thousand shares at par."

"Yes, quite right," said Rodney, as Peale's head disappeared.

"Who the deuce is that, Rod?" asked Mr. Smith briskly.

"Oh, one of my staff," said Rodney carelessly. An idea was rapidly taking shape in his head, and he felt that he was carrying through his scene quite cleverly.

"One of your what?" asked Mr. Smith amazed.

"My staff; I've gone into business," said Rodney.

"You've done what?" asked Mr. Smith, laughing uproariously.

"Gone into business. I'm a business man," repeated Rodney.

"That's the funniest thing I've ever heard of," said Mr. Smith.

"What's funny about it?" asked Rodney, beginning to feel hurt.

"You — in business!" Mr. Smith laughed again.

"It's true, though, and as a business man I'd like to talk to you," Rodney went on, "regarding a very interesting business proposition in which I am now interested."

"Nothing doing," said Mr. Smith, quite frigidly.

"I thought I'd like to borrow ten — say a few thousand dollars," said Rodney gulping.

"No, sir; not a cent," said Mr. Smith.

"Perhaps five thousand," amended Rodney.

"If it was for a new club or some tomfoolery, in a minute; but to put into your business — it'd be just throwing it away. Why don't you get your father to back you?"

"Father and I don't agree on the value of advertising."

"Oh, that's it, and you expect me to do what your father won't?"

"Well, I thought as a friend of the family," stuttered Rodney.

"You were wrong. Where is your father?" asked the friend of the family.

"In there I guess," said Rodney.

"I want to see him. I guess he'll think this is as funny as I do," Mr. Smith laughed, going out, leaving Rodney sunk dejectedly in a chair.

"Well?" asked Peale coming in again.

"He wouldn't give me a cent," said Rodney.

"He wouldn't? Well, he sounds like your father's oldest friend."

"What about the Countess?" Rodney inquired.

"Oh, I got *her,*" said Peale proudly.

"You did? Ten thousand dollars?"

"Fifteen thousand."

"Holy jumping Jupiter."

"Pretty good, what?"

"Good? Why, why — I'll have to raise your salary," said Rodney.

"Thanks — I supposed you would," said Peale complacently.

"Where's the money?" asked Rodney.

"We don't get it till next week," explained Peale.

"Oh," said Rodney dejectedly. "But we must have some more cash to start with."

Peale meanwhile must have left the ladies in some suspense, or else they missed his cheery company, for presently Mary came back and said the Countess wanted to know how much longer she must wait.

"Coming now," said Peale. "Shall I sign for you?"

"Sure — sign anything — sign it twice," said Rodney.

"You know this has got the show business beat a mile," Peale chuckled, as he disappeared.

Money — what an awful thing it was, reflected Rodney. Why was it never there when you wanted it, but plenty of it in the bank for some old tight-wad who couldn't enjoy it? He turned to Mary fondly, wondering if there were not some way in which they could raise some immediate cash: but Mary failed him now for once. She hadn't an idea, she admitted sadly. But in the meanwhile Mr. Smith had emerged from the inner office, and something must have come over the spirit of his dreams of good investment, for he greeted Rodney very genially and encouragingly this time. Rodney introduced Mary to him with great pride, catching her back as she turned to go.

"That's all right: you needn't go, Mary. Mr. Smith, this is the future Mrs. Rodney Martin."

"You don't say so," cried Mr. Smith heartily. "Well, well, congratulations."

"I suppose you and father had your laugh at me," said Rodney.

"No, I didn't tell him anything," replied Mr. Smith.

"Thanks for that anyhow," said Rodney.

"Of course it sounded funny to me at first," pursued Uncle William, "but when I thought things over, after all, why shouldn't you be a success in business?"

"What?" said Rodney, hardly able to believe his ears.

"You've been successful in everything else you've tried," said Mr. Smith, without a hint of sarcasm.

"Yes, yes, certainly, sure," said Rodney.

"Of course you haven't tried much, but as you said, I am an old friend: and I figured if you gave me your word that you'd return the money within a year, perhaps after all it would only be the act of an old friend to take a chance. That's what friends are for," explained Mr. Smith.

"Why, that's simply great of you, by George," said Rodney.

"How much was it you wanted?"

Behind his back the delighted Mary held up the fingers of both hands.

"Ten thousand dollars," said Rodney promptly.

"But didn't you say —?" queried Mr. Smith.

"Oh, I'm sure I said ten thousand dollars," Rodney declared. "That's the very least."

"Um — well, I'll mail you a check to-night," said Mr. Smith.

Mary could not repress a squeak of delight, which caused Mr. Smith to look sharply at her a moment. Rodney interrupted again with his thanks, speaking enthusiastically:

"I'll never forget it. I tell you, friends do count. Thanks, thanks."

Mr. Smith for some reason seemed quite emharrassed.

"That's all right," he said. "Don't thank me. Good night, Miss Grayson, and I hope you'll be very happy."

"Good night. Good night," echoed Rodney as Mr. Smith went out. "Oh, Mr. Smith, have you your car with you?" he added anxiously. "Tell the chauffeur to drive slowly and carefully."

Left alone Rodney grabbed Mary by her two hands and danced around excitedly.

"Ten thousand, and he lent it to me. Oh isn't it great?" he shouted. He kissed her on the strength of it.

"Wait till I tell Peale," he cried and slammed out.

In the meanwhile the Countess came back, her shrill French voice sounding through the door long before she appeared. "Oh, c'est une affaire magnifique. Je vous remercie. Oh, les Americains," et cetera, et cetera, she rattled on, as she was bowed out into the hall to the elevator.

"What did she say?" asked Mary of the French maid.

"She said the American men are splendid, but the women are crazy and they can all go to the devil."

"Oh," said Mary, rather shocked. Who would ever have believed that chic and fascinating countess, so Frenchy and interesting, could be guilty of such vulgar sentiments? Mary wondered if Marie had not colored things a little in her translation. What was Marie doing down here in the office anyway? The French, at any rate when you employed them as servants, were always intriguing for some purpose or other. She couldn't have come to see Mr. Martin, for she had not gone near him, or asked to see him. Mary made up her mind that she had come down out of curiosity about Rodney, pure and simple.

She recalled at last that she was to report to Mr. Martin herself. She went up to the door of his private room and knocked discreetly three times. The old gentleman came in promptly in response to this concerted summons.

"Well, how goes it?" he asked.

"Oh, Mr. Martin, he's perfectly splendid," said Mary enthusiastically. "So full of energy, hustle and ideas. He's a different man already. You were right; he only needed development."

"Good. Good," said Mr. Martin. "You're not saying this to flatter an old man's vanity, are you?"

"Indeed I'm not," said Mary. "We don't have to blast."

"Would you rather take a guarantee of twenty-five hundred dollars additional and give up that ten per cent. of his profits?" he asked shrewdly.

"I should say not," said Mary.

"You know, Miss Grayson, you're making me believe we'll win that thirty thousand from old John Clark."

"Oh, indeed we shall. You should have just seen Rodney borrow ten thousand dollars from Mr. Smith, without the least trouble."

"Oh, that was my money," said Martin smiling. "When Smith told me Rodney tried to touch him

— well, I thought the least I could do was to back my own son, so I sent Smith out to make good with him."

"That was nice of you," said Mary, outwardly polite, but inwardly disappointed at the deception.

"Well — I owed the boy a chance anyhow," said Martin, softening a little, then suddenly talking very sternly again as he caught sight of Rodney through the open door.

"So you're still hanging round, are you?" he grumbled, facing his only son relentlessly.

"Yes, sir, but I came to see Miss Grayson," said Rodney, coming in to his father perkily. "Come, Mary," he added to the new secretary.

"Really going into business, eh?" scoffed his father. "Well, when you fail don't come sniveling back here. You can't count on a dollar from me. You're leaving my employ of course, Miss Grayson."

"I won't snivel — and I don't want your money," retorted Rodney. "I don't need it. Why, if I'd known how easy it is to raise ten thousand dollars I'd have gone to work long ago."

Mr. Martin, senior, grinned at Mary.

"You would, eh? Well, what soft easy going business have you picked out?" he inquired sarcastically.

"The soap business," said Rodney.

Mr. Martin, senior, was genuinely annoyed.

"What? Why, you can't make any money out of soap."

"Oh, yes, I can."

"I control all the important soap business in the country."

"I know you do but I am going to take it away from you."

"What?" roared Mr. Martin.

"Yes sir, I'm going to manufacture the 13 Soap," began Rodney spouting his piece, "unlucky for dirt — the most expensive soap in the world. I'm going to break the trust — I'm going to attack monopoly. I'm going to appeal to the American people for fair play against the soap trust. You've always wanted me to go into business. Well, I'm in, and forgive me, father, but I'm going to put you out of business. I'm going to advertise all over the world."

"You can't fight the soap trust with advertising — we're established," said his father coldly.

"Yes, yes, we can," said Rodney; "think what advertising means; the power of suggestion — the psychology of print. Why, ninety-seven per cent. of the public believe what they're told, and what they're told is what the other chap's been told, and the fellow who told him read it somewhere. Advertising is responsible for everything."

Ambrose Peale came in during this tirade and stood listening, surprised and pleased with his pupil's aptitude.

"People are sheep and advertising is the way to make 'em follow your lead," went on Rodney, trying not to forget the speech. "Say, what makes you go to the theater? I'll tell you. It's what you've read of the play, or what some fellow's told you, and the fellow that told him read it in a newspaper. And, that, father, is the whole secret of it. You've got to be talked about. Get 'em praisin' or cussin', but don't let 'em be quiet. I want to tell you — Say, what kind of duck's eggs do you eat?"

"What!" cried Mr. Martin, aghast.

"Do you know anything against the duck?" shouted Rodney. "No, you don't; but when a duck lays an egg it's a damn fool and keeps quiet, but when a hen lays an egg — Cluck, cluck, all over the place. Advertising!"

Peale joined the chorus on the old gentleman's off side, and together they talked such a blue streak that Mary put her fingers in her ears. If she removed them she was assailed by old Mr. Martin's angry denunciations, for this rival company was not at all, it seemed, what he had bargained for. She preferred to stop her ears, and with her eyes behold Rodney and Peale gleefully spouting their psalm of advertising, and shaking hands with each other like long lost friends.

CHAPTER VII

BUSINESS AND LOVE

CHAPTER VII

BUSINESS AND LOVE

AND so the new 13 Soap Company was launched; — or perhaps one should say merely that the keel of the new craft was formally laid. There was a good deal about it to be built up and finished off yet. From the beginning, however, it was all a joy to Rodney; it gave Mary's lover something sweet to work for, and the sense of responsibility grew stronger in the boy the more he dwelt on it. For her sake he would make good, and not for his father's money. Mary and he were really partners, and saw each other every day, which was almost the best part of it. Sunday was the one dull day of his week, for then he didn't see her till afternoon, and not always then. The secretary and treasurer of the 13 Soap Company was a woman, and clever enough to know that distance lends enchantment and absence makes the heart grow fonder — sometimes.

Rodney went to her not only for love and kisses, but for advice and encouragement too, and there were many details to be thought of in the course of the first few weeks. Even Ambrose Peale admitted that they must have an offiee, though he denied that there was any necessity for making real soap, at any rate just at present. Mary and Rodney were appointed a committee of two on getting an office. To Rodney there was some sentiment in this matter of domiciling their business, of giving it a home, so to speak. It was a delightful occupation to the ex-millionaire's son when both members of the committee, Mary and he, went out together on the hunt. The next month of his life was one of the happiest he had ever spent. The rickety elevators that they rode in, the janitors they interviewed, the real estate agents who lay in wait for them, were minor annoyances compared with the pleasure of taking lunch with Mary in some queer restaurant when the noon hour came. Her level head and unfailing good sense were a support and comfort to him that he came to appreciate more than he would have believed possible. He had loved her for a long time, and now he liked her too. Besides his passion for her there was now the even firmer bond of friendship. If only he could be sure that she loved him as much as he loved her. His own heart beat for her in so many ways; did hers respond always? He tortured himself exquisitely with his doubts these days, Mary was so demure and serious, so very unsentimental sometimes.

One day they were enjoying a fifty cent table d'hôte at a place on the West Side, not far from the borders of old Greenwich Village, that Faubourg which has lately blossomed out as the Latin Quarter of New York. They had found the lofts further up town too expensive, Mary insisted, and as their business was to grow into a big wholesale business, as Rodney said, if they didn't land father, they did not really need to locate in the Fifth Avenue section. And they simply must economize, Mary protested: a small business must economize just as much as an individual with a small purse. Besides it would leave more money for the ads.

The lunch place was one to which, traditionally, you needed to be introduced, and Mary and Rodney had come there first under the escort of Ambrose Peale. To-day they were alone. Good old Peale, thought Rodney; but he mustn't get interested in Mary.

Puccelli's was one of those places where the food was meager, and the atmosphere rich. In the summer months you ate in the backyard, with a faded awning over you; in the winter you sat at a table in what had formerly been the front or back drawing-room, with sliding doors of pressed glass that were made to divide the two apartments. The food was always the same: a tray of nondescript hors d'œuvres that were meant to execute a reconnoissance in force on your appetite and divert its main attack elsewhere; a soup that was about the color and savor of rain water; a portion of chicken that must have been consanguineous with some species of centipedes, so inexhaustible was the supply of drumsticks; — the whole topping off with a thimbleful of ice-cream and two lady fingers. There was also usually a bottle of red wine, which Rodney used to say was filled with the same juices as those big globes in chemists' windows, and which had the same decorative effect when the sun threw its colors on the thin and spotted table cloth.

This impressionistic view of the place was the way at least that it struck Rodney first, fresh from the ministrations of Johnson and the soap king's chef in the mansion opposite the Park. Later he came to judge it less intolerantly, to know that for poor people, and he was now enrolled among the poor, New York was a choice of inconveniences. He never tried the wine, but the food, from association with Mary, began after a while to taste good to him. He was with Mary, and he did not sigh for his father's house: "better a dinner of herbs where love is than a stalled ox and hatred therewith."

Puccelli's centralized a portion of New York that was as strange as Europe to Rodney Martin. It was wonderful how much of your surroundings you didn't see if you lay on the small of your back in a racing car when you went through them. The very look and smell of the locality were different from other portions of New York; there was a different complexion on things too, for red brick prevailed as a building material, and the sun warmed it more generously in this district, where skyscrapers had not yet begun to sprout and soar.

Mary had the idea at one time of establishing their business in an old house, and she and Rodney passed in and out through the portals of many a deserted mansion in the old Greenwich or Chelsea purlieus. It was curious what a variety of architectural and decorative effects had been obtained in the set arrangement of these old formal dwellings. The long pier glass between the two front windows, the carved marble mantelpieces on every floor, less elaborate as you neared the attic, were different each from the other, though the family resemblance was a marked one. There was one really stately mansion, not far from the piers of the new Chelsea Improvement, where the great red and black funnels of the

Cunard steamers towered above the warehouse roofs at high tide, which gave Mary and Rodney quite a thrill as they entered it. It was four or five stories high, and a very spacious staircase rose upward straight away from the front door. Splendid Doric columns marked off the drawing-rooms, and there were elaborate and tasteful cornices for each story. Not a sign of legend or tradition or romance stamped the whole, as it would have done in Europe; it had just been the home of some forgotten rich man of that time, some soap king maybe; but on this account the two lovers and business partners felt it as all the more their own. This mansion and all the others they looked at were invariably exhibited to them by some furtive landlady, and examination of the premises showed that she eked out her rent, which was not so very low, by stowing the young men, her lodgers, away two in a room; and there was always a notice of "Furnished Rooms," written in ink on a piece of cheap note paper and glued to brown stone or brick at the right of the front door bell.

"It's no fun being poor," said Rodney; "is it, Mary? I don't wonder you want me to work. But I'm working for you, not the money, mind!"

In the end they gave up the scheme of a house and went back to lofts. In a house you would need a janitor and coal in winter, as Mary decided finally, and you could get more for your money in a loft.

To-day at lunch Rodney was in a fairly sentimental mood, and he felt somehow that Mary didn't respond to him as she ought. He tried to get hold of her hand beneath the table cloth, but she avoided him. There were tall thin stalks of bread on the table, standing upright in a glass like celery, and tasting, when you got a piece between your teeth, more like raw macaroni than proper bread. It was one of the specialties and bits of local color at Puccelli's; but Mary couldn't really pretend she liked it, he was sure, to eat. Mary herself looked good enough to eat, to-day, thought Rodney, as he gazed at her across the rickety little table, her pretty white teeth crunching the bread strongly and heartily.

"Mary," he said at last; "I want to ask you something."

"Yes, Rodney."

"Do you love me as much as you did?"

"Yes, Rodney."

"Could you love me any more than you do?"

"Yes, Rodney."

"Do you know that I love you more every day of my life?"

"Yes, Rodney."

"Mary!" he exclaimed; "are you paying any attention to what I'm saying, at all?"

"No, Rodney."

She broke one of the bread sticks in two with a brittle crack, and handed a piece across the table to him. He seized it and her hand too, eagerly; he didn't care who saw. As a matter of fact no one saw, excepting old Madame Puccelli in the caisse, who looked on, benevolent and approving. He held the warm little hand in his and tasted the thrill of it, looking straight into Mary's gray eyes, and hoping he made her veins too run a little faster than their wont.

"Mary," he said at last, "have you seen father lately?"

"I saw him the other day driving through Thirty-fourth Street. He had the car stopped and spoke to me."

"What did he say? Anything special?"

"Why, no; nothing special. He only scoffed a bit, and condoled with me, as much as to say we were going to the dogs, of course, eventually."

"More soon than later, I suppose," sighed Rodney. "Do you know I have often wondered what the old man thought of you, Mary?"

"Of me?"

"I think he liked you, the old rascal," declared Rodney openly. "That's what I think. I think you could have been the second Mrs. Cyrus Martin if you had wanted to be. It's coarse of me to say that, I suppose."

"Indeed it is, Rodney. What makes you say it?"

"Oh, a lot of things; and do you know I think his firing you after I left the house was a bluff? He did not really seem very angry with you that last day there in the office."

By a strange turn of affairs Rodney had begun to have fits of being jealous of his father where Mary was concerned, and he could feel one coming on now. The trouble had been intensified by his chance discovery that Mary's five thousand dollar contribution to the new company's capital had been in the form of a check signed by the elder Martin. He had teased her about it, at first playfully, and she had told him she would tell him nothing except in her own good time; that he must trust her meanwhile. There is always a little rift like this within the lute, a crumpled rose leaf in the bed, a question that Psyche must not ask of Cupid; only in this case the sexes were reversed, and it was the lad and not the lass that must contain his curiosity. Rodney began again, a little less playfully, a little more vexed as his mind dwelt on it:

"Why should he hand you over a check for

five thousand dollars if he was angry with you?"

He watched her jealously while he made this last speech, and thought she looked particularly conscious at the mention of the check to-day.

"It was a good joke our starting a rival business with the pater's money," he continued, "but I wish to goodness it hadn't come through you."

For an answer Mary began to pull down her veil and make various feminine movements to indicate that she had had enough, and was ready to go. She was leaving her ice-cream and lady fingers untasted.

"You're absurd, Rodney," she vouchsafed. "Pay the bill now and come along. We must meet that man about the partitions at two o'clock."

Rodney paid and came along as he was bidden. They tramped eastward together without a word, and arrived in the empty loft before the carpenter.

Miss Burke, the new stenographer, and Peale, had not come in yet from lunch. It took but one glance to assure Rodney that he and Mary were alone.

"Mary," he said quickly, drawing her closer to him, "forgive me! I'm a cad."

"Why, there's nothing to forgive, you silly," said Mary. "Now this partition here should be —"

"I don't think there should be any partition

between you and me," interrupted her lover warmly. "Prove that you forgive me by giving me a kiss. It's only the eleventh I've ever had."

And without waiting for an answer he took her greedily in his arms and pressed his lips to hers for a long and rapturous minute. If that counted as one kiss his eleven had not been so far from riches after all.

"Rodney," cried Mary, breaking away at last, "there's the elevator door. Some one's coming."

It was Ambrose and Miss Burke coming back from lunch, but Rodney was too full of his love's intoxication to care whether they had seen the eleventh kiss or not, either of them or both.

The offices of the Soap Company were finally located about half way down Broadway. There was a waiting-room, and a private office — as private as could be expected with three people using it. It was a rather commonplace room, furnished comfortably but not elaborately. The walls were hung with posters extolling the virtues of 13 Soap, such as,

DO YOU BELIEVE IN SIGNS?
13 Soap is Unlucky for Dirt

BE CLEAN
Cheap Soap is For Cheap People

13 Soap is the Most Expensive
Soap in the World—
one dollar a cake

One particularly large stand on one wall bore the legend:

The average cake of soap
gives you 56 washes
A Cake of 13 Soap
gives you only 24
BUT
WHAT WASHES!

There was a door on the left of the room and also two more on the right. At the back were windows through which the callers could see the building across the street literally covered with 13 Soap posters.

There was a desk in the middle, and there were chairs, cabinets, a hat rack, a water cooler, a safe, etc., which completed the equipment. The water cooler was much appreciated by the various errand boys, who were its chief patrons. Mary thought it a little extravagant to supply them with so much of it, but the cooler looked well, and so it remained in its place.

"Experience is a dear school," says Poor Richard's Almanac, "but fools will learn in no other, and scarce in that." The 13 Soap Company's experience began at the bottom—to wit, with office boys.

Up to that time no one connected with the company had realized the infinite varieties of the genus office boy.

There was the mulatto boy, recommended by the Methodist Sunday School, who began his career by stealing a dollar's worth of postage stamps. Though he wept and blubbered in contrition when his theft was discovered, even the tender-hearted Mary turned her thumbs down and declared that he must go. It was not safe, in a business concern, to have any one around who was not absolutely and religiously honest, she argued; and though there was not much yet in the way of loose change to make away with, the principle prevailed and the mulatto boy went.

There was the boy who was always being absent for Jewish religious festivals, and the boy who in spring, when the good American's fancy lightly turns to thoughts of baseball, buried at least three grandmothers without a tear. There was one full grown boy who confessed at the end of two weeks that he was a little off in his head, and begged them not to give him too much work. There was a boy whom the agents of the Gerry Society came and carried away with them, and one cherubic little applicant that Mary almost cried over, he seemed so tiny and tender. To Rodney the sight of his sweetheart with this plump little morsel of human young in her arms gave a thrill that resolved him upon working all the harder for the good fortune that was in prospect for him. Luckily for the company these boys, good, bad and indifferent, went as mysteriously as they came — ephemeral insects that swarmed awhile in the hot air that rose from the soil of this business world and disappeared.

Mary drew a great argument for woman's suffrage from the ease with which they obtained a good stenographer. Miss Burke, not so many years older than the oldest boy, came quietly, and as quietly conquered the job. You would have said she had had the benefit of years of experience, whereas she had only the trick of keeping her mouth shut and her eyes open.

Ambrose Peale noted with regret that the new typist was distinctly plain. Miss Grayson had turned away others that were much better looking, he thought, whether Rodney noticed it or not — but he didn't — and Ambrose made a mental note of the circumstances.

In a month from the time Rodney had left his father's house and embarked on his business career with Ambrose Peale there was a very fair show of activity in the 13 Soap Company's office. There was a fairly large mail — mostly circulars — which the entire office staff read through every morning, for lack of more interesting reading matter in the way of orders. Discipline was not yet rigorously enforced by anybody. Next to the circulars the largest part of the mail was invitations forwarded to Rodney from the Fifth Avenue address uptown. In her capacity as secretary Mary, with her woman's curiosity, ran her steel envelope slitter through these too, and sighed sometimes as she opened up some especially attractive bit of cardboard to think of the joys that Rodney had turned his back on.

CHAPTER VIII

THE GREAT CAMPAIGN

CHAPTER VIII

THE GREAT CAMPAIGN

RODNEY'S back was turned on his old life now,— there was no doubt of that. The boy was usually the first after Mary to reach the office. Peale was always late.

" I say, Peale," Rodney would say, " you're late again. It's got to stop. Here it is ten o'clock."

" Don't scold, little boss," Peale would answer, as he hung up his coat. " That blamed alarm clock — first time in my life it didn't go off."

" I'm afraid that's old stuff," Rodney would answer sternly.

One morning Peale looked at the little boss in great surprise.

" Holy Peter Piper, you've shaved off your mustache," he ejaculated.

" Yes," said Rodney, grinning, " I'm just beginning to get on to myself. By George, I certainly used to look like the devil. Do you observe the clothes? " he added, rising and turning round.

" Why, you're getting to be a regular business man. My tuition," said Peale.

"You bet your life. Business is great fun," said Rodney. "I thought it would bore me, but it's immense; it's the best game I ever played. What's the news with you?"

"Well, I've been on father's trail," answered Peale. "We only just got back from Buffalo this morning."

"We?" queried Rodney.

"Yes, your father and I," Peale explained. "He went to the Iroquois in Buffalo. I had all the billboards in the neighborhood plastered thick — and forty-eight street stands along the streets to the Union Station; from the time the old man got in until he got out, he couldn't look anywhere without seeing 13 Soap. I even found out the number of his room, and had a small balloon floating 13 Soap streamers right outside his window. I took a page in all the Buffalo papers — bribed the hat boy to keep putting circulars in his hat every time he checked it — and sent him one of our new folders every mail. I came back with him on the train, and when he went into the washroom last night I had the porter say, 'Sorry, sir, we ain't got no 13 Soap, but you can't hardly keep any on hand — it's such grand, grand soap.'"

Another day Rodney allowed that all they had done was great business along the line of their drive at father, but he had a fine new idea, too.

"When you go into a barber shop, where do you look?" he asked Peale.

"At the manicure," said Peale promptly.

"No, no, at the ceiling," Rodney explained. "We'll put signs on all the barbers' ceilings."

"It's been done," said Peale scornfully. "Is that what you call a great new scheme?"

"Well, that wasn't my big idea," Rodney hedged.

"No; well, what is your big idea?" inquired Peale mockingly.

"Plans for our new factory," Rodney answered.

"Plans for what? Have you gone dippy?"

"Here they are," said Rodney, producing a large blue print. "Pretty real looking, aren't they?"

"You don't mean you've actually got some nut to build us a factory?" shouted Peale.

"No, no, they are to impress father; don't you see?"

"Oh — yes; well that is an idea," admitted Peale.

"If he ever does drop in to make a deal," said Rodney, "I thought we ought to have something to make a front; something that looks like a plant."

"Plant is right," averred Peale.

"And by the way, if we can, let it leak out that

it's the Ivory Soap people who are backing us with unlimited capital," went on Rodney.

"The Ivory Soap people?" Peale inquired.

"Sure, father's always hated 'em in business," explained Rodney. "His oldest friend, though, is John Clark, one of the big bugs in Ivory Soap. Clark's got a son Ellery that father dislikes because he's such a success in business; — always held him up to me as a model son to pattern by. It would make father wild if he thought that old Clark was going to back us. Ivory Soap's the only bunch he's never been able to lick —"

"Then that scheme ought to be good for a great rise out of father. Say, by the way, I put over a corner on him this morning," chattered Peale. "I arranged for a parade of sandwich men up and down in front of his house. When he got to his office there was another bunch there."

"We're bound to land him sooner or later," Rodney agreed; "keeping after him the way we have."

"Just as sure as it pays to advertise," said Peale.

"Isn't it funny, though, that nobody's tried to buy any soap from us yet?" asked Rodney with some anxiety.

This was a very tender point with the soap company. Mary and Rodney worried over it, and Rodney dreamed at night about it. An occasional small order that might filter in from some remote outlying district, or some small merchant whose credit was doubtful, was gazed upon as parents gaze at their first baby. Peale was the bachelor of the crowd, and seemed not to care whether they were productive or not.

"It takes time to create a demand," he would say; but admitted that the two hundred cakes of pink castile they had bought looked swell in their old rose wrappers. It was a pity they hadn't got a couple of hundred thousand dollars to go after this advertising thing on the level, instead of just for father. Neither he nor Rodney knew how much money they had left.

"Don't ask me," said Peale. "I'm not a financier. Where's our worthy book-keeper, Miss Grayson?" he added, looking at his watch. "It's nearly eleven."

"I'll bet she was here before either of us; she always is. By George, isn't she a corker?" began Rodney lyrically.

"Oh, she's all right," agreed Peale indifferently.

"All right! Why, the girls you read about don't mean anything compared to Mary," began the ecstatic lover. "She's got Juliet beat a mile. Every time I think of her I want to yell or do some other darn fool thing, and every time I see her I just want to get down and kiss her shoes."

Rodney said all this and could have said much more, but Peale's mind was on other things.

"If we could only land one hard wallop on father after that Buffalo business," he reflected sadly, still on business.

"Didn't you hear what I said?" demanded Rodney indignantly.

"Not a word," said Peale.

"I was talking about Mary."

"I know you were. That's why I didn't listen," said Peale delicately.

"Speak of the goddess," he added, as Mary just then entered.

She was dressed neatly and appropriately to her new rôle, distinguishing between the tone of the old Martin offices and this new enterprise into which she had been drawn by such curious processes. To Rodney as always, this morning and every morning, she was a vision of loveliness, a refreshment for tired eyes.

"Ah, you're here," he said joyfully; "now everything's all right; it's a great world."

"Don't be silly," said Mary briskly; "this is a business office."

"By George, Mary," began Rodney again.

"Miss Grayson!" corrected Mary.

"By George, Miss Grayson, you do look simply

stunning. You're twice as pretty to-day as you were yesterday, and to-morrow you'll be —"

"Hey, hey, change the record, or put on a soft needle," put in Peale good-naturedly. Mary rewarded him with her approval.

"Quite right — in business hours only business," she said.

"But you certainly are the prettiest thing," persisted Rodney.

"Am I?" said Mary.

"Well," said Peale, "it looks to me as if you two were going to play another love scene, so I shall attend to a little business. Exit advertising manager up stage," he laughed, going out.

"By George, Mary, it seems a hundred years since yesterday — I do love you," Rodney began again, when they were alone.

"Do you really?"

"Why, of course."

"It isn't that you're just in love with love," suggested Mary with a thoughtful look, "and that I've been very blue-eyed and baby-faced?"

"I should say not," protested Rodney. "Why, you're not a bit like that."

"Oh! Why do you love me, then?"

"I don't know."

"You see?" said Mary accusingly.

"I mean why does anybody love anybody," Rodney expounded. "I can't explain. It's just that you're you, I guess. I can't talk the way they do in books; I wish I could. All I know is that if you left here I'd quit too. I'd just want to walk around after you all the rest of my life and say, 'Are you comfortable, my love? Are you happy?' If there is anything on the wide earth you want let me get it for you, Mary. What a wonderful name that is — just like you; simple and honest and beautiful. Mary!"

"And you really love me like that?" asked Mary.

"No. A million times more."

"Oh, Rodney, Rodney," she said, almost crying.

"What's the matter," asked her lover anxiously. "You love me too, don't you?"

"It means a lot to me to see you succeed," sighed Mary.

"But it isn't just the success — just the money, is it?" queried the boy.

Mary paused a while and then answered, "No, I don't think it is."

"Then when will you marry me?" he began eagerly.

"Not in business hours —"

"Very well, we'll wait till after six."

"No, you agreed not until you'd made good."

"I know, I know, but it's mighty hard to be engaged and not to be allowed to kiss you. You won't even let me come to see you — much. It's all just business. Do you love me?"

"Do you doubt that I do?"

"No, but I'd like to hear you say you do."

"I won't gratify your vanity. We must stick to soap and advertising. Is that understood?"

"I suppose so, for to-day anyhow," he agreed, then leant over and kissed her suddenly.

"Oh, Rodney," protested the secretary.

"They say stolen kisses are sweetest, but I don't think so," he said, laughing. "They're so darned short. Won't you give me a real one?"

Mary shook her head.

"No — now to business."

Rodney sat down again with an air of resignation.

"Well, then if this is a business office, what do you mean by not getting down here till nearly eleven?" he demanded sternly. He did not really think she had been remiss; he was only teasing her, of course. He was the optimistic one, and knew things were all right. Peale had hypnotized him with his advertising magic.

It had been great fun reading the "ads." They had seemed so large and conspicuous and inescapable. You would have thought that every reader of the newspapers, every traveler in the cars or busses in the special section marked out by Peale for old Mr. Martin's benefit, would have ordered 13 Soap straightway next morning, whether they needed more toilet soap or not. Rodney had positively a feeling of self-consciousness as he walked down town in the morning. There was a half formed thought in his head that he might even be pointed at in the streets as the president of the great 13 Soap Company. Now Mary's grave face and her cool ways when he would have made love to her chased all such business reveries into thin air.

"I was here at nine," said Mary.

"I knew it. But where've you been?"

"That's what I've got to tell you. I'm sorry it's such bad news."

"It can't be very bad if it comes from you."

"But it is — I've been out trying to raise money."

"Why, Mary, are you in trouble?"

"No, but I am afraid you are."

"If you wanted money why on earth didn't you come to me?" asked Rodney.

"Because you haven't any. This firm's broke."

"But we can't be."

"I was surprised too when I balanced the books this morning," said Mary; "but you've spent a lot these last two days. Here's a statement of assets and liabilities — you owe twenty-two thousand, eight hundred and eighteen dollars and nine cents."

"Great Scott — what are our assets?"

"One hundred and thirty-three dollars and thirteen cents."

Rodney shook his head courageously.

"That's quite a showing for a month," he chaffed.

"And Mr. McChesney, the advertising man, was here this morning too. He won't wait any longer for his money," went on Mary.

"But we paid him five thousand dollars not long ago."

"And we still owe him nine thousand four hundred," said Mary. "Unless he gets two thousand five hundred of it to-day, he says he will put you out of business."

"You didn't manage to raise any money while you were out, did you?" Rodney asked, pocketing his qualms about the source of Mary's capital.

"Not a cent," said Mary. "And you haven't heard from the Countess since that day she signed the contract?"

"Not a word," said Rodney, and added hopefully, "but maybe we shall soon."

"I don't know what we're going to do," said Mary, sighing.

But Rodney was still hopeful and inclined to cheer up.

"The important thing is, I've got you anyhow," he said happily, just as Ambrose Peale came in again.

"Well, well, well, still spooning, eh?" said Peale. "Say, son, I've just learned a lot from that advertising agent down stairs. Great little guy, full of facts and figures. He gets paid fifty thousand dollars a year for writing ads."

Peale was incorrigible, and to-day his talk, in the face of their actual condition, got on Mary's nerves a little. She interrupted impatiently.

"Never mind him," she said to Rodney, "we're broke."

"Nonsense — some mistake in the books," said Peale.

"Is it? Here's a statement of our liabilities," she said, holding up a paper: "twenty-two thousand, eight hundred and eight dollars, and nine cents."

"What's the nine cents for?" Peale wanted to know, reading. "Assets one hundred and thirty-three dollars and thirteen cents. That's a lucky hunch — thirteen — well, why not change the headings? Make the liabilities the assets and the assets the liabilities. See, like this," and he scribbled on a pink pad that he carried with him:

"Liabilities, one hundred and thirty-three dollars and thirteen cents; assets twenty-two thousand eight hundred and eighteen dollars and nine cents — merely a matter of book-keeping," he added cheerfully, jabbing the pink paper on a hook.

"You'd make a wonderful expert accountant," said Mary scornfully.

"And McChesney's coming here to-day for money — cash," Rodney put in, trying to take Peale down.

"He is? Well then we won't do any more business with him," said that incorrigible.

"No, I guess we won't," repeated Mary sardonically.

"He's got to have twenty-five hundred immediately," continued Rodney.

"He has, eh?" said Peale. "That's the trouble of dealing with business men. They're so particular about being paid. Now you take actors —"

To Mary and Rodney, however, the thing seemed serious. If McChesney did give them any financial publicity it would finish them with Rodney's father. Peale told them not to worry. They would fix father somehow. Nobody could stop good advertising. Why, honest, he used to think he knew something about ads, but after he'd talked to this fellow downstairs for ten minutes he learned more than he ever had dreamed of. And believe him, he was a pretty good dreamer too.

"You really think we ought to go right on spending money advertising?" asked Mary.

"Sure. That's all we can do," said Peale. "Why, the Ingersoll people advertised a year before they put the dollar watch on the market — just to create a demand. That's our game."

"But it's mighty expensive," Rodney objected. "You said we could last a month on twenty thousand dollars."

"I know, I know," said Peale, "but these things always cost a little more than you figure on."

"A little more!" echoed Mary, flourishing her statement.

"I suppose we might as well owe forty thousand as twenty," said Rodney.

"Certainly, and as a matter of fact we're pikers," said Peale. "We haven't really been spending anything. Why, if we just had the money — but don't get me started on advertising. You know me."

"Go ahead — I shouldn't mind hearing something cheerful," said Rodney.

"Cheerful," said Peale. "My boy, advertising's the most cheerful thing I know. It can do anything but keep you from coming into the world and going out of it."

"I'd believe in it more if we were making money," said Mary.

"Patience, dear lady, patience," Peale counseled. "Did you ever hear of the National Cloak and Suit Company?"

"No," said Rodney.

"I have," said Mary.

"You see, she has," said Peale. "Well, the guys that ran that company suddenly thought of a scheme — Tailored suits by mail.— See, measure yourself." He measured his chest. "Thirty-six, see." He measured his waist. "Forty-eight. That kind of thing. New idea in the business — absolutely. Fitting women they had never seen. Everybody laughed at 'em — couldn't be done. Why? Never had been. Gee, that's a great argument, isn't it? But they plunged — spent all of three hundred dollars right in a bunch. That was ten years ago. Last year they spent three hundred and fifty thousand dollars advertising and sold a million suits to a million women they never saw. What did it? Advertising."

"And you know when Bryan advertised the grape juice high ball," Rodney added quizzically, "its sale went up six hundred and fifty-two gallons a day?"

"Nix, nix, I'm not pulling any of that stuff now," said Peale. "This dope is on the level."

"It's hard to believe," sighed Mary.

"And yet it's true," Peale maintained; "but that's nothing. What do you think the Victor Phonograph Company gave up last year for advertising?"

"A hundred thousand dollars," said Mary.

"Two hundred thousand dollars," said Rodney.

"You're warm, you're warm, both of you," said Peale. "One and one half millions. Fifteen hundred thousand dollars, ladies and gentlemen."

"On a phonograph? That's ridiculous," said Mary.

"That couldn't pay," Rodney protested.

"Of course it couldn't," Peale mocked. "Their gross receipts for the year were only sixty-six million dollars, and each year they spend more money and sell more machines and more records. Why, in nineteen hundred and seven, during the panic, when everybody had cold feet and began to shut down, they appropriated an extra three hundred thousand dollars on publicity, and what happened? No, they didn't increase their sales, but they kept them right where they were, and when lots of other businesses were going broke they continued naking money."

"All this is mighty interesting," Rodney admitted.

"I never dreamed people spent that much money advertising," said Mary.

"Neither did I," said Peale; "and say, when you talk about our piking liabilities, do you happen to know what real advertising costs? Ever hear of the *Ladies' Home Journal?*"

"Sure," said Rodney, smiling.

"Ever read it?"

"I should say not," said Rodney indignantly.

"I read it every month," Mary admitted.

"You see," said Peale triumphantly, "she reads it. The women all do, and they tell the men what they've been reading. Men may not read the *Ladies' Home Journal,* but they hear about its ads — word of mouth advertising."

"Granted — but what's the point?" asked Rodney.

"You read the *Saturday Evening Post,* don't you?" demanded Peale.

"Sure. Philadelphia's biggest export," said Rodney.

"Exactly. Well, the *Ladies' Home Journal* and the *Post* are run by the same publishers. *Journal* twice a month and *Post* once a week. Their receipts from advertising in 1913 were one million dollars a month — and do you know what they charge for space? The back page in the *Journal* costs for one insertion ten thousand dollars, for the *Post* seven thousand, and as the *Post* comes out weekly that means twenty-eight thousand a month. Of course, if you want a measly inside page, that's just a trifle of forty-five hundred."

"It's too amazing," came from Mary upon this information, and from Rodney the mystified query:

"And they really get those prices?"

"My boy," said Peale, "the back page in the *Journal* is taken for the next two years. People are fighting now to get in the 1916 Christmas issue. That's how far ahead they lay out their campaigns, and that's another funny thing about advertising. You'd think once a trademark was established it would last, but not a bit. You've got to keep plugging. Remember Spotless Town?"

"Sure — Sapolio, wasn't it?" asked Rodney.

"I knew the girl who wrote the ads," said Mary.

"Well," said Peale, "after a while they quit on it, and then Sapolio's sales went way down; but now I hear they're going to revive Spotless Town this year and try to come back. But it would have been so much better if they'd never gone away."

"You're not stringing me in all this?" put in Rodney skeptically.

"No. I got it all from this guy — and he knows. Think what a great trademark we've got; and he says that's seventy per cent. of the battle. Do you remember Sunny Jim?"

"Certainly — I can see his picture now," said Rodney, and Mary remembered him too.

"What did he advertise?" Peale demanded.

But neither Rodney nor Mary remembered that, they said.

"Exactly," said Peale. "Well, he advertised a breakfast food called Force."

"Oh, yes, of course."

"But you forget that," Peale explained, "and that was why Force canned Sunny Jim. He was the thing that stuck by you — the advertising was more important than the goods. You remembered Jim, but you forgot Force. Bad publicity. And that's where we've got the bulge. The 13 Soap — it's great — it's got imagination — Soap — a fact — 13, unlucky — unlucky for what? Why, dirt. Imagination, superstition, humor. Cleanliness, soap — all associated in one phrase. Plus buncombe, good old bunk for the pinheads — the most expensive soap in the world. And think of the advantage we have that we're selling soap. People know whether automobiles go or not — if clothes wear well, or collars crack, or soups taste good, or furniture falls apart, or roofs leak, or phonographs can't talk. There you have to deliver the goods; — but soap or dental cream, or tooth powder or cold cream, who really knows anything about 'em? Who can tell anything about 'em? Can you? I can't. All you have to do is to make 'em smell nice."

Rodney began to take fire again from this enthusiasm.

"By George, it's wonderful, colossal, I never realized it," he began.

"Neither did I," assented Mary.

"Kind of beginning to believe in advertising?" buzzed Peale.

"More than ever; but then you convinced me the first time you talked about it," said Rodney.

"Then don't go up in the air, either of you," said the ex-press agent, "when I mention that while I was downstairs just now I got that fifty thousand dollars a year chap to promise to write some ads for us. I signed a contract for ten thousand dollars' worth more space."

"Good Heavens!" cried Mary.

"I didn't know then we were broke," said Peale, assuming the defensive.

Rodney, with Mary's figures fresh in his mind, wondered where the money was coming from, but Peale was equal to that too.

"From father," he said; "when we've created

a big enough demand he just can't help coming in with us. That's business."

Mary hoped so, and as for Rodney he was growing more and more enthusiastic, and chimed in:

"I know so. By Jove, if other people can do those things by advertising we can. We'll keep on. We'll manage somehow."

"I like to hear you say that," said Mary, quieting her doubts.

"Now you're talking," said Peale; "you're going on spending money on publicity, and that's my idea of real conversation."

Once more the enthusiasm of Ambrose Peale carried the day. Mary pocketed her statement and her qualms as best she could, half believing he was right, as she looked at Rodney's irradiated face.

Of course the question of capital had not even yet been quite solved. Why wait till it was all paid in, objected Peale, who had been too eager to begin to wait for a detail like that. Rodney's one thousand, and the money from the car and aeroplanes, Mary's five thousand and the ten thousand from William Smith had come in and gone out again, by the time Mary's statement was made up. There remained only the Countess and her money to look forward to for the present and the immediate future, and she was expected soon.

CHAPTER IX

SOWING THE WIND

CHAPTER IX

SOWING THE WIND

ONE day, sure enough, not long afterward, Miss Burke tripped into Rodney's office and handed him something which had not yet become common in the company's routine — namely, a letter with a foreign stamp and postmark. The three partners were standing about as usual when this dramatic little incident occurred. Mary was willing to bet it was another bill, and Peale asked what odds she was giving: would they be as high as one hundred to one? Rodney in the meantime, who had opened the epistle and been reading it, shouted out:

"Hurrah, hurrah, it's from the Countess!"

They had pinned their hopes to the Countess's Parisian skirts, and here she was coming back again in the nick of time; luck was with them.

"What does she say?" asked Mary, much excited, while Peale grabbed the letter and exclaimed in disgust, when he had glanced at it, "Oh, French stuff."

"She says she was delayed abroad — but that

she's due on the Imperaytor, or rotter, this morning, and that she's coming to see us at eleven."

"It's half past eleven now," Mary sighed. "Oh, dear. She's late."

"Fear not," said Peale. "Remember, though a countess, she is still a woman; give her time."

"Does she say anything about the fifteen thousand dollars?" asked Mary, to which Rodney was obliged to answer No.

Peale, however, had a hunch everything was going to be all right. Unluckily Miss Burke punctured it by entering and saying Mr. McChesney was here to see him and seemed very angry.

"My hunch is wrong," said Peale. "Here's where we take an aeroplane and dig a hole right through the ceiling."

"Keep a stiff upper lip," Rodney counseled.

"Oh, sure, I'm full of starch," Peale retorted.

"Good luck, Rodney," said Mary.

"Don't worry — I've got a way to square him," Rodney answered.

They had looked forward to the Countess and her ten thousand dollars, and instead here was McChesney again with his advertising bill. Such were the ways of business life. A colorless, unprepossessing person enough was McChesney, but in truth the soap trio would have been poor judges of any man's personal magnetism who came on

McChesney's errand. To them he was just the man with the advertising bill.

He entered quite boldly, allowing he'd come right in and not wait to be told they were all out. He was an experienced bill collector.

There was nothing to do but receive him bravely.

"Why, hello, Mr. McChesney," said Rodney genially, pretending to be quite glad and surprised to see him.

"How are you, Mac—" began Peale. He even tried to shake McChesney's hand, but was thrown off roughly.

"You may be in the soap business, but cut out the soft soap with me," was his unsympathetic comment. "Where's my money? Have you got it?"

"Why — er — the fact is —" Rodney began.

"That means you haven't."

"Well, you see —"

"Bury the stall, bury it," said McChesney, brutally. "Do you think you can put me off? You can bet your blooming liabilities you can't. I'm going after you good. I think this whole concern is bunk and I'm on my way to the sheriff now."

Rodney grew provoked.

"I don't care for that kind of loud talk. Drop it," he said sternly.

"Drop it," repeated Peale.

"What?" exclaimed McChesney in surprise.

"He said drop it," repeated Peale.

Rodney stumbled on:

"It's simply that I haven't had time to examine your bill in detail. This afternoon, however, I —"

"Old stuff — old stuff," McChesney scoffed.

But something gave Rodney a new resolve.

"Meanwhile," he went on, "I'll give you a check for two thousand five hundred on account," he said. "I presume that will be satisfactory, won't it?"

"Why — yes — sure — but —" McChesney stammered, taken aback; and Rodney turned to Peale and added:

"You understand, Mr. Peale, that not a cent of that fifty thousand dollars we appropriated for our October advertising campaign is to go to him?"

"Absolutely," said Peale. This was a great word with Ambrose, pronounced always with a strong accent on the "loot."

McChesney was impressed.

"Now, Mr. Martin, I'll admit I'm hasty tempered. I'm sorry I made a mistake, but a contract is a contract, and —" he began.

"Here's your check. Good day," said Rodney.

"But, Mr. Martin —"

"Show Mr. McChesney out," Rodney went on to Peale, who obeyed with glee.

"Come on, Mac — this way to the elevator," he said.

Poor Mary had observed this scene with renewed dismay.

"Oh, dear," she said. "You've only got us into more difficulty. You know there's not money in the bank."

"But the check won't go through the clearing house until to-morrow morning, and by then we'll have the ten thousand dollars from the Countess," protested Rodney.

Peale looked at his watch and wondered where the Countess was.

"I'll bet she sank in mid-ocean," he predicted dolefully. Wasn't that just the way with money when you wanted it? So things always went, it seemed, when they needed cash. They had looked forward so eagerly and so long to that fifty thousand francs, and instead they had entertained a dun, a very vulgar and demonstrative dun at that.

Rodney could not pretend he liked such scenes, and said so with some vigor. Even Peale looked a little sympathetic, and forgot to spout his advertising gospel.

It was adding injury to misfortune when a card was presently handed to the President of the 13

Soap Company bearing the name of Ellery Clark. How Rodney hated that fellow! He must admit that Ellery had never done anything to him, but he could not hear him, just the same. He said as much to Peale, whose curiosity seemed to be aroused:

"Let's have a peek at him," he said.

"Take a good look at him," said Rodney as Miss Burke went after Ellery, "and see what father wanted me to be like. Ellery went into business — so must I. Ellery loved work — so must I."

"But it was only his pride in you," said Mary. "Your father didn't want old John Clark constantly rubbing it in about Ellery's success."

"I didn't want it rubbed into me either," said Rodney.

"Well, this is our chance to impress Ellery," said Peale. "Who knows, too? He may have some money."

"Meanwhile I'll go call up the steamship office, again," said Mary. "Oh, Rodney," she called back, "find out how Ellery's doing in business, will you?"

Rodney watched her as she disappeared, and was brought to presently by Peale.

"You're spoiling that girl — she used to be a good business woman. Now, half the time instead of using her brains she sits and looks at you as if you were some marvelous antique work of art."

Rodney laughed, and as a matter of fact liked this teasing. Above all it was delicious to his heart to hear Peale say that Mary was in love with him. He did think Mary was beginning to show a little more love for him lately, despite their troubles, and Peale's testimony made him glad. He looked up quite good-naturedly, only forcing a frown on his face as Ellery Clark came in. Ellery bored him awfully at most times.

The truth is John Clark's Ellery was a real pin-head, and always would be, overdressed in the latest style, affected, aping the English when he remembered to do so, but oftener than not forgetting.

"Hello, Rodney, mind if I come in?" he called out cheerfully.

"I'm very busy to-day, Mr. Clark," said Rodney coolly.

"Oh, I suppose you are," Ellery agreed. "Must take a lot of time to get up your advertisements."

Peale pricked up his ears at this.

"You like 'em? I write 'em. My name's Peale," he rattled off, coming over to Ellery, who, however, looked right through him as if he were empty air. That sort of treatment was lost on

Ambrose, who only walked back to his chair, comically rebuffed, and settled down to the rôle of listener.

"What is it, Mr. Clark?" Rodney went on.

"You see, it's like this, old top," said Ellery. "I've been having rather a time with father lately. Silly old man. Of course with a dad like yours, who's perfectly satisfied with you, you can't understand that."

"No, of course not," said Rodney dryly.

"You see, my old man's out of date," Ellery went on, encouraged. "Insisted on the absurd idea of my going into business — beastly bore."

"But you wanted to, didn't you?" asked Rodney.

"I should say not."

"But I thought you loved work?"

"Work? It's preposterous, except for the lower classes. Men of intelligence go in for the professions. I paint."

"You look it," said Peale, in a half aside.

"I'd heard you were a model son," said Rodney.

At this Ellery opened his eyes and stared.

"Why, that's just what father says about you," he exclaimed. "He says you're a great executive."

"Well, I must admit that business life is very congenial to me," said Rodney, mussing up some papers on his desk and employing his rubber stamp vigorously.

"Oh, I don't consider it a compliment to be a success in business. Think of all the blighters who are," declared Ellery.

"Yes, the bally rotters," Peale interjected, unable to keep still. He had been observing Ellery all this time as if fascinated by this new specimen. Unconsciously he began to mimic him. If Ellery crossed his legs he crossed his. He even took his handkerchief and stuffed it in his cuffs like Ellery.

"Father keeps reminding me of your success every day," said Ellery plaintively; "most irritating. Of course he's sore because I haven't bothered much about business. Oh, I've tackled a thing or two; but luck was against me — just didn't happen to work out. Not my fault, you understand."

"I should say not — you couldn't be to blame," came from Peale, who must talk.

"Of course if I'd really devoted myself to business," Ellery went on; "but when you know you can do a thing if you want to, why bother to do it if it bores you?"

"Good idea that," echoed Peale.

Ellery proceeded to explain that his father had been particularly offensive lately, so that he had decided to give a little time to business and make a success of it. He could, you know. It was really quite simple. Oh, quite. He had things all figured out. For the scheme he had in mind he had got to raise seventy-five hundred dollars, and he wanted to talk about it. Peale and Rodney exchanged looks.

"I'm very sorry, Ellery," Rodney answered, "but money's tight just now."

"But not with you," said Ellery. "The way you're working you must be pretty rich. Heaven knows you ought to be — manufacturing soap."

"But all my capital is invested already," explained Rodney. "I can't undertake any outside ventures. Can I, Peale?"

"Not with my consent," Peale agreed. "You ought to see our assets and liabilities."

But Ellery went right on:

"This idea of mine is an automobile proposition. I really need ten thousand dollars, and I've only got two thousand five hundred."

At the mention of this latter sum Rodney and Peale walked over to Ellery at once, and stood one on each side of him, like a state coat of arms. Money! They took a good look at him.

"Ellery, why do you want to go into the automobile business?" began Rodney genially. "It's dangerous — unsafe —"

"The risk's tremendous," Peale corroborated.

"Ellery, our families are old friends," said Rodney. "Now if you really want to show your father you're a money maker, why don't you buy some shares in our company?"

"I don't care much about the idea of being in the soap business," Ellery protested; "rather vulgar."

"But you don't have to be in the business," said Rodney eagerly.

"Absolutely not," said Peale.

"It's a very simple proposition," Rodney began again. "All you do is invest, and then sit still and deposit your checks when we pay dividends."

At the word dividend Ellery gave a pleased smile.

"I say, that sounds a bit better," he agreed.

"We're not letting the general public in," Rodney explained; "but it would be such a joke on your father for you to make money."

"Yes, wouldn't it?" said Ellery with a vacuous laugh. In fact they all laughed.

"I fancy he'd be mighty glad I had sense enough to go in with you," added Ellery. "But is it a safe investment?"

"Why, we'd guarantee you against loss — wouldn't we, Peale?" said Rodney.

"Absolutely," said Peale, with a strong accent on the loot.

"From our assets," said Rodney.

"From your assets?" asked Ellery.

"Yes, here's a statement," Peale went on, taking his pink version of Mary's statement off its file.

"Twenty-two thousand eight hundred and eighteen dollars," Ellery read off from it, holding it in his gloved hand.

"And nine cents," added Peale.

"That sounds rather ripping," Ellery admitted. "Should I have to do any work?"

"You work? I should say not," said Peale.

"Of course," added Rodney, "before I can promise to let you in Mr. Peale would have to agree."

"Do you agree?" asked Ellery, addressing Peale for the first time.

"Oh, yes, I agree — I agree," said Peale, perhaps a shade too quickly.

"Now what do you say, Ellery?" asked Rodney, trying not to appear too anxious.

Ellery put the silver head of his cane in his mouth and sucked at it a long time.

"I'll do it," he said at last.

"God's in His Heaven. All's right with the world," chanted Peale.

"Have you the money with you?" asked Rodney, his heart beating.

"Why no," said Ellery, opening his eyes.

"Then you'll send us a check to-day?" put in Peale.

But Ellery wouldn't get the money until next week, it seemed. His father hadn't promised it till next Monday. He couldn't ask him for it now, you see. Ellery was afraid he couldn't really. His father was out of town.

"But we can't agree to hold the matter open until next Monday," said Rodney firmly.

"No, not till way next Monday," Peale agreed. "Why don't you telephone him?"

Yes, that wouldn't be so distressing, Ellery thought. If he could get him it would be considerably easier to talk to him on the phone. He could always ring off then.

"Come this way then — it'll be quieter for you if he's noisy," said Peale eagerly, leading him to a booth. "Never mind the social chatter," he added, as Mary came in and Ellery stopped to talk with her. "Ellery, you don't mind my calling you Ellery — do you, Ellery? You see, Ellery has work to do," he went on for Mary's benefit.

"It's very pleasing to find you both so beastly charming to me," said Ellery.

And that was a model son, thought Peale. Thank God he was a black sheep himself. That was always the way with money; it was never in the right hands.

Meanwhile there was still another chance, for Mary informed him that the Countess's boat had docked three hours ago.

"Oh, Rodney, by the way," she asked, "did you find out how Ellery's doing?"

"He's doing great," said Rodney. "Hasn't made a cent. Wanted to borrow some money from me."

"Your father would be glad to hear that," she laughed.

"Where *is* our wandering Countess?" sang Peale, just as Miss Burke came in and announced:

"The Countess de Bowreen."

"By golly, she's entering on the cue," said Peale joyfully.

"We're safe now," said Rodney.

"Oh, I do hope so," sighed Mary.

Money!

It took some maneuvering to manage the coming Countess, with her ten thousand dollars, and Ellery with his prospective twenty-five hundred. They needed either or both of them to cover up that twenty-five hundred they had handed to McChesney. Mary and Rodney dared not think what would happen if new capital could not be obtained in time.

Then just as the Countess was about to be shown in the capable Ellery stuck his head in the door and vowed he could not manage the telephone: he never had run a switchboard: he was not good at mechanical problems. Mary was told off to ring up his father for him, and Peale called after her to hold his hand, or kiss him — anything to leave the floor clear for the Countess; — needless to say the kiss was not suggested by Rodney.

Rodney ran to a window and pulled down a shade on which was blazoned:

SAVON TREIZE
PAS BON
POUR
LE SAL

He turned round to greet her full of hope. He was sure he could understand anything she said about money. He would leave to Ambrose the pleasant sensation of spending it on advertising.

When she finally swept in he met her with a delighted air and kissed her hand, which was the way in which he had conceived the part. He also said Bonjour, twice, and pointed to the shade that bore the French advertisement.

The Countess gave a little shriek of appreciation and declared it was magnificent, superb. She was desolated to be so late, but things had been very complicated at the customs. Rodney could make out also that she inquired if they had received her letter? Peale had been listening intently and couldn't keep still.

"Oh, you little life saver," he chirped.

He, too, kissed her hand, on Rodney's telling him it was French stuff. She looked like money, Ambrose thought. She must have it.

"Ask her, ask her!" he whispered to Rodney.

"Have you the money?" Rodney asked her nervously, thus enjoined.

"Eh?" said the Countess.

"Come on, kid, say yes, say yes," whispered Peale, snapping his fingers.

"Vous-avez l'argent?" Rodney began.

"Oui, oui, j'ai de l'argent," said the Countess.

"What does she say?" asked Peale anxiously.

"She says yes," interpreted Rodney.

Peale gave a suppressed squeal of delight.

"Shall I kiss her?" he asked.

"The money with you?" Rodney asked again.

"Eh?" said the Countess.

"L'argent avec vous?" said Rodney.

"Oui, j'ai de l'argent ici," responded the Countess, opening her bag and taking out a check.

" It's real," said Peale in a hushed voice.

" C'est un cheque de Morgan Harjes pour cent mille francs," said the Countess.

" Draft for twenty thousand dollars," Rodney interpreted swiftly.

" Slip it to me, kid, slip it to me — I'm dying on my feet," cried Peale, as the Countess jabbered off a few dozen words again to Rodney.

Rodney explained now that she wanted to send the draft to the bank to get it cashed: that she was not known there; and that she would give them their fifteen thousand.

" I'll make a world's record getting it cashed," said Peale, and reached greedily for the check. The Countess pulled it back, however, in surprise, and only gave it up again when Rodney explained that his manager was going over to the bank. Peale grabbed it, then paused, dramatically.

" Say, wait a minute," he whispered hoarsely.

" What is it? " asked Rodney.

" Why don't we stall the Countess off? " suggested Peale.

" What for? " asked Rodney.

" Why, borrow the money from her, and keep the whole twenty thousand for a couple of days. Get me? "

What followed this speech gave Ambrose Peale

one of the biggest surprises of his life. The Countess had been watching the conversation eagerly, like a bird, turning her head quickly from Peale to Rodney as they spoke, and looking very innocent and chic. Upon the finale of Peale's scheme to " borrow " her money she broke out into perfectly good American.

" Why, you cheap grafter! " she cried indignantly, with a real Bowery accent.

" She spoke English! " cried Rodney, and the Countess suddenly covered her mouth with her hand, realizing for the first time that she had given herself away.

" Suffering cats, she's a fake," Rodney added.

Poor Ambrose was hardly able to speak:

" And the draft's a phoney too," he ventured.

The Countess agreed, shrugging her shoulders.

" Sure it is. Gee, you were easy. If I hadn't lost my temper." It was curious the entire change that had come over her.

" Well, you're frank anyhow," Rodney said to her.

" Why not, it's all cold now."

" What was the game, kid? " Peale asked her, taking a professional interest.

" I was going to trim you for the five thousand dollars change from that draft," said the Countess.

"Great Scott!"

"But why pick on us?"

"I didn't start out to; you wished it on yourselves," said the Countess. "I came to trim your father. You remember I wanted to see him,—but I looked so soft you thought you'd grab me off and sell me the French agency of your 13 Soap. I didn't think your father could be as big a boob as you were, so I changed my plans. Do you get me?"

"Yes, I get you, and now I'm going to get the cops to get you," said Peale sternly.

"I should burst into laughter," cried the Countess. "Why, you pikers, I'm on; you're busted. You haven't got any money, and you have got a phoney company."

"Now, see here," expostulated Rodney.

"Preserve it, preserve it," the Countess interrupted. "Don't forget I've understood everything you two guys were talking about."

"Whew!"

"Gee!"

She proceeded to give them a little scene to illustrate. To Rodney she said:

"Kiss her hand — it's French stuff."

To Peale:

"Ah there, you little life saver."

To Rodney:

"The money with you — l'argent avec vous? Gee, your French is rotten."

To Peale who moved away from her:

"Shall I kiss her?"

Then she added after a pause:

"Send for the cops and I'll blow the whole thing to the papers."

She rested her gloved fingers coolly on her umbrella handle and surveyed the two boys.

"Well, I guess we're quits. If you had any money I'd ask for a piece of change to keep me quiet. But as it is I can't waste my time."

"You're not French at all?" Rodney queried.

"I was educated over there. Immense, wasn't I? You never tumbled at all."

"But why the foreign stuff?" Peale inquired.

"Well, I can talk good French, but my English is punk," explained the Countess.

"You won't say anything now?" Rodney pleaded.

"No, I don't hit a fellow when he's down. Anyhow we're all in the same class. Three fakes. I'll keep mum if you do."

Oh, money, money!

So much for the ten thousand dollars. The twenty-five hundred was no nearer, as was presently to appear, when Ellery Clark stuck his head in the door, grinning, and asked to see Rodney a moment. Peale could not help noticing the change that had come over the countenance of Ellery.

"You seem very beastly pleased, Ellery," he said. "Is everything all right about father?"

"Oh yes, so to speak, in a way," said Ellery, still grinning.

"What do you mean, so to speak, in a way?" Peale demanded, suddenly suspicious.

Oh, money, money!

And Ellery explained. The trouble was that Ellery couldn't get father on the telephone, and that did make it so much easier, Ellery thought. He did not fancy talking to father about money: that was the truth, and he couldn't get father, because father was off on Long Island Sound somewhere with his yacht, and wouldn't be back till Monday. Apparently Ellery was relieved by this unavoidable postponement, and so he grinned and thought it was all right.

Poor Ambrose, thinking of the twenty-five hundred dollars, thought it was all wrong.

The Countess, taking in the general appearance of Ellery, thought something might be doing, for she eagerly and promptly dropped her handkerchief. Ellery pounced upon it at once, handing it to her with a flourish.

"Is there no one to take me to my taxi?" she

cried next. It was a general invitation which Ellery accepted on the spot.

"These American buildings are so big I am lost," she went on, with a more marked accent than she had used a moment ago.

"Ellery, you take the Countess," suggested Rodney, willing now to get rid of them both.

"Oh, I'd love to," said Ellery. "I say charming, what?"

"Madame la Comtesse de Beaurien — Ellery Clark," said Rodney, introducing them.

"Dee-lighted," cooed the Countess.

"So am I," said Ellery, adding audibly, "Ripping little filly."

"You speak the French?" the Countess purred, as they went toward the door.

"No, not at all," said Ellery.

"A pitee."

"But I can speak German."

"Aber prachtvoll — ich liebe das schoene deutsche."

"Ich auch —"

"Warum laden sie nicht zum Biltmore zum Thee ein?"

"Mit dem grossten —"

"Vergnuegen?"

"Yes," said Ellery, relieved, "that's the word — vergnuegen."

"Au revoir, Mr. Martin," said the Countess, looking back at Rodney over her shoulder. "Vous êtes trop aimable. Je vous remercie beaucoup de votre politesse. Au revoir." Then in her American accent she added to Peale in an undertone. "So long, kid, call me up sometime."

And chattering a stream of German to Ellery she went out.

In fact it all went, the twenty-five hundred and the ten thousand together. Peale viewed the two departing figures sadly, with mixed emotions. She was a ripping little filly indeed, that "Countess," as that silly ass Clark had said, but the silly ass was having a ride with her now in a taxi, and the clever man, Ambrose Peale, was staying behind worrying about his advertising bills. Oh, money, money!

CHAPTER X

A VISIT FROM FATHER

CHAPTER X

A VISIT FROM FATHER

DURING this trying month old Cyrus Martin, the soap king, had sat in his library in Fifth Avenue, or in his swivel chair at his office, and wondered how things were going with the boy anyway. From such information as reached him, he was not so encouraged as he would have liked to be. A month was not long enough to tell, of course, in the normal course of things, but that fool advertising made another matter of it. Those huge billboards and electric signs and balloons and sandwich men: piffle, all of it, but Martin knew what such things cost, and was sure that Rodney's company could not possibly stand it. He was worried. And he was annoyed too. These abominable sandwich men; he had had one set of them arrested that afternoon on the Avenue. He couldn't stand it. People might know who were in this ridiculous 13 Soap Company, and he should be well laughed at.

Another and contradictory thing was the rumor he had heard down town yesterday that the Ivory

Soap people were backing Rodney's company, going to build a plant for them. In fact putting one thing and another together he decided he would drop down and give the boy a call at his office. It wouldn't be bad to see him again, and Mary Grayson too. So he presented himself at the new soap company's office, on Broadway, and was kept waiting for his pains. A Miss Burke took in his name and he guessed that it caused some excitement, for he could hear Rodney's voice and another's chatting inside while he cooled his heels. It was a foolish thing to keep important visitors cooling their heels: Rodney should have known better than to do that.

When he was at last ushered in the place looked like a real office, on the whole, and there at a desk sat Rodney, talking through the telephone; his father caught something about "not considering it," and "not having any stock for sale"—"quite out of the question," et cetera, et cetera, as he took a chair.

"Well, well," thought Mr. Martin, rather pleased and proud. "What's this?"

Rodney in a moment dropped the telephone and espied his father.

"Why, hello, father," he greeted him genially.

"Hello, son," said Mr. Martin. He observed with astonishment that Rodney was very busy filing papers, opening and closing drawers, and that every now and then he signed a typewritten letter viciously with a rubber stamp.

" Sit down, won't you? " said Rodney presently. " I'll be with you in just a moment."

" Thanks," said his father drily.

" Have a cigar? " said Rodney, handing the old gentleman a box in an absent-minded way.

" Thanks," said Mr. Martin, biting off the end and lighting it at the match which Rodney held for him. Rodney lighted one too.

" Surprised to see me, I suppose," said his father presently.

" Not a bit," said Rodney, flourishing a contract and signing it. Mr. Martin had some curiosity to see what it could be, this thing which really looked like a contract, but his son turned it upside down and blotted it ostentatiously on his desk pad.

" There, that's done," he added. " Now, father, what can I do for you? "

" Well, my boy," said Mr. Martin. " I just dropped in for a social call. The fact is I've rather missed you."

" I've missed you too, father," said Rodney.

" Thought I'd have a look in and find out how things were going," said Mr. Martin abruptly.

" Fine — fine," said Rodney, " everything breezing right along. Of course, I'm always glad to see you," he added, pushing the buzzer, "but right now, father, I'm pretty busy, so you'll excuse me if —"

He got very busy indeed again with his papers.

"Well, if you can spare the time, I'd like a little business talk with you, Rodney," said Mr. Martin, with a certain sarcasm.

"Certainly, in just a minute," said Rodney, still preoccupied with his papers, but pricking up his ears.

Ambrose Peale, coming in, stopped suddenly when he saw who their visitor was. Rodney looked up at him.

"That's all right, come right in," he said. "Father, you remember Mr. Peale? Peale, my father —"

"Indeed yes, I recall very well —" began Peale effusively.

Mr. Martin gruffly cut him off.

"How are you?" he said.

"A bit tired," said Peale, sitting down comfortably; "just back from Buffalo where we're conducting a big campaign."

"Is that so?" said Martin, senior, crustily.

"Perhaps you've heard about it?" inquired Rodney, looking at his father.

"No. Why should I hear about it?" said that gentleman for Peale's benefit especially.

"I don't know," said Peale helplessly.

"You see, Mr. Peale handles all our advertising, and perhaps —" began Rodney.

"Oh, he does — does he?" said Mr. Martin dangerously. "Then it is to him I should address myself."

"Either or both of us," chirped Rodney.

"Then both of you listen to me," Martin began. "You've got to cut out this nonsense you call advertising —"

"What nonsense?" asked Rodney.

"Yes, what?" echoed Peale weakly.

"This morning there was a parade of sandwich men in front of my house for two hours," Mr. Martin went on indignantly. "I had to have them arrested. I got to the office to find another bunch. It annoys me."

"I'm sorry, father," said Rodney.

"You're trying to make a fool of me," said his father. "I open a letter. It's a circular for 13 Soap. I open my newspaper — you have a page ad. I look out of the window — there's a billboard. I take a train — the damned porter apologizes because he's all out of 13 Soap."

"Well, of course, all that proves how wonderful our publicity is," said Rodney bravely.

"You're a grand young bluff, my son," said Martin grimly.

"Why, father, what do you mean?"

"I'll tell you exactly what I mean. I've let you ramble on to see just how far you would go, but you've been spending a lot of money advertising, hoping that by annoying me I'd buy out your business to get rid of you. Well, I'm not going to. Now what have you got to say to that?"

"Nothing — absolutely nothing," said Peale, taking heart again, and Rodney resumed quickly:

"But I have — a lot to say. We may not have a big business now, but we have got a trademark: — the catchiest trademark ever invented for Soap. We're a growing concern. Just because our advertising annoys you you mustn't think it's valueless. Why, it's so good that capital is chasing us.— Our money is practically unlimited.— Is that a fair statement, Peale?"

"Very fair — very fair, indeed," agreed Peale, dazed at Rodney's daring.

"Bluff, son, bluff," Mr. Martin repeated.

"Not at all," protested Rodney, "and since you're so skeptical, father, I don't mind letting you see the plans for our new factory."

"New factory?"

"Yes, father. These are the offices. Here is the power house, and this is my office, and here is Mr. Peale's —"

"Aren't you going to make any soap?"

Rodney looked blank.

"Who's putting up the money?"

"Now, father," said Rodney reprovingly, "you cannot expect me to divulge a business secret to you, a rival manufacturer."

"Oh, why not tell him. He is your father," said Peale nobly.

"Well, Peale, if you really think it's wise?" said Rodney.

"Oh, yes, I think it's quite wise," said Peale.

"It's the Ivory Soap people," declared Rodney boldly.

Mr. Martin was at once impressed and annoyed.

"The Ivory Soap people," he repeated, flicking the ash from his cigar.

"Yes, the Ivory Soap people," echoed Peale, rubbing it in.

"You mean John Clark?" asked Mr. Martin, getting out of his chair.

"Yes," said Rodney.

"Absolutely," said Peale.

Mr. Martin turned and reflectively walked up and down. Peale very obviously picked up a push button and pushed the buzzer twice. There was a pause and then in a moment Ellery Clark stuck his head through a door on the left. Mr.

Martin did not know it, but this was all by prearrangement with Ellery. Peale, when he had come in just now, was fresh from tutoring Ellery in a little speech. The idea was to impress Mr. Martin overpoweringly on the subject of the Clark family's connection with the new factory. But Ambrose was, to tell the truth, a little nervous as to Ellery's ability to overpower the soap magnate. Ellery's first idea too seemed to be of bolting.

"Oh, excuse me, I didn't know your father was here," he began politely.

"That's all right, Ellery," said Rodney very genially.

"Yes, come right in," said Peale.

Ellery came in.

"How do you do, Mr. Martin?" he inquired.

"How are you, Ellery?" Mr. Martin responded gruffly.

He didn't like all this, but what was the matter with Ellery?

"Well, I really can't wait any longer," began that youth. "The party down stairs in the taxi — you follow me?"

"Yes, Ellery, you told us that," said Peale, shutting him off.

"Well, good-by, then," said Ellery.

"Was that all you came in to say?" Rodney

took him up hastily, looking at Peale, and Peale added sharply:

"Yes, have you decided about that deal?"

Ellery's mouth fell open, and a look came over his face as of one remembering a lesson.

"Oh, of course. If you'll keep it open until Monday I'll have the money for you then," he said.

"But we can't wait till Monday," said Rodney.

"But Mr. Peale told me —" Ellery answered, puzzled.

Peale came quickly to his rescue:

"We'll see what we can do, but just now, Ellery, we're very much occupied," he said, taking him by the arm and starting toward the door.

"Oh, just a minute," said Rodney. "You'd better give your father back the plans — say they're quite satisfactory."

"What plans?" queried Ellery helplessly.

"Oh, didn't he tell you about them?" Peale put in. "Perhaps after all, Rodney, I'd better give them to Mr. Clark myself. You remember I have an appointment with him to-day?"

"Oh, yes, it was to-day, wasn't it?" said Rodney.

"But father's out of town," Ellery protested.

"I know he is — otherwise I could have kept the appointment," said Peale.

"We'll give you a definite answer to-morrow," added Rodney.

"But I don't understand," Ellery persisted; "really now, you say one thing and Mr. Peale came in and —"

But already Peale was leading Ellery gently and firmly to the door.

"We'll have to see you later in the afternoon, Ellery," he said politely.

"But what did you want me to come in for?" quavered Ellery.

"Don't you see?" said Peale.

"No —"

"That's too bad; — well, good-by, Ellery."

"I say, I do find business very confusing — I prefer the Countess," murmured Ellery, going out.

"Ellery talks too much," said Rodney when Peale came back.

"He is very indiscreet," Peale agreed; "if it had been anybody but your father he'd have given our whole plan away."

"What's he doing here — acting for his father?" inquired Mr. Martin. His ideas of Ellery were undergoing a change.

"Absolutely," said Peale.

"You're not going to take him in," said Mr.

Martin, "that pinhead? Why, he didn't even seem to know what he was trying to get at."

"No, he didn't, did he?" agreed Peale.

"But after all, he does represent Ivory Soap," said Rodney.

"Great soap — Ivory — ninety-nine and forty-four hundredths per cent. pure," said Peale.

Mr. Martin grunted. There was something funny here, some kind of play-acting, though he couldn't quite make out what it was. Old Clark's Ellery was a fool; you could see that with your eyes shut. Yet a fool made a good go-between sometimes, and you never could tell what John Clark would be up to. Ellery sounded for all the world as if he were trying to recite some piece that Rodney and that fellow Peale had taught him. And yet what did he happen to be doing there in the 13 Soap Company's offices? That couldn't have been prearranged. John Clark was up to anything. Cyrus Martin made the mistake that shrewd men often make of attributing too much subtlety to his rivals. The idea of cutting the whole thing out was taking shape in his mind; it came to the same thing whether he was fighting Clark or Rodney. If he bought Rodney out the boy could be said to have made money in the year's time that had been set for the wager, and in that case whatever he paid for the fool concern would be reduced by thirty thousand dollars. And those awful sandwich men!

As he paced up and down the office, revolving these ideas in his head, he caught an exchange of gleeful glances between Peale and Rodney. That decided him.

"Ivory Soap!" he grunted. Then to Rodney, in a more propitiatory tone, he added: "Have a cigar?"

Rodney took one of his father's Havanas and threw away his own stub.

"Thanks," he said.

There was a pause.

"Have a cigar, young fellow?" said Mr. Martin to Peale next.

"Thanks," said Peale, surprised.

"Allow me," said Mr. Martin, lighting his cigar and then walking over to Rodney.

"Well, thinking things over, why should you and I fight?" he began.

"You started it, father," said Rodney.

"Quite true," said Martin, "and therefore I should be the one to call it off. Now, son, here's the idea: — I'd rather have you with me than against me — the money doesn't matter much. In your way, while I don't endorse that kind of publicity, I suppose you boys have done some good advertising."

"Thank you, sir —" chimed in Peale.

"Not at all," said Martin; then added to Rodney, "and if you're going to have a hacker, shouldn't I be better than the Ivory Soap people?"

Rodney's throat gave an involuntary cluck of pleasure.

"After all, blood is thicker than business; what do you suggest?" he said.

"Suppose I buy you out," Mr. Martin said; "including your trademark and good will?"

"Oh, you have our good will, now, sir," put in Peale.

Rodney reflected:

"Buying us out might be expensive for you, father."

"Oh, I guess it won't take all the money I've got; — what's your proposition?"

"What's yours?"

"How is the business — what are the assets and the liabilities?"

"How fortunate! It was only this morning that Mr. Peale roughly copied off the totals from our books," said Rodney.

"I try to keep up with every detail of the business," chirped Peale.

Rodney passed out the pink statement.

"There you are, father," he said.

"Hm, liabilities one hundred and thirty-three dollars and thirteen cents — assets twenty-two thousand eight hundred and eighteen dollars," read Mr. Martin.

"And nine cents," added Peale.

"That's a remarkably good showing," admitted Mr. Martin. "Well, I'll give you fifty thousand dollars for your business as it stands."

Rodney took a good hold of himself.

"But we don't want to give up our business," he protested; "I like business. I wish you'd made me go into it years ago, father."

"We wish to continue in our chosen profession," added Peale grandly.

"Well, suppose you take twenty-five per cent. of the profits," suggested Mr. Martin.

"It's wonderful weather, isn't it," said Rodney; "these crisp, cold, bracing mornings."

"Well, I hardly thought you'd grab at that," said Martin; "what will you take?"

Rodney rose to the occasion quickly.

"One hundred thousand dollars cash," he said; "you assume all the contracts and obligations of this company, give us forty per cent. of the profits, a contract for me at twenty thousand a year, for Miss Grayson at ten thousand"— Peale coughed audibly behind him—"and another for Mr. Peale at the same figure."

Mr. Martin looked at the two men a moment, chewing his cigar:

"Done," he said finally. He could see, out of the corner of his eye, Peale and Rodney exchange looks and shake hands. Well, he had come down to buy them out.

"I congratulate you, father," Rodney said.

"You needn't," said Mr. Martin. "As a business proposition I don't think much of it, but I guess it'll show old John Clark he can't butt into my family affairs or get Ellery mixed up with my boy's business."

"Yes, father, we'd much rather have you than Ellery," asserted Rodney.

"Oh, much rather," echoed Peale.

This important deal was no sooner agreed on than Miss Burke came in inopportunely, and conveyed to Rodney the information that the agent of the landlord wanted to see him: indeed that he wanted to see him immediately.

"Yes," said Rodney. "You see, father, we're thinking of taking larger offices," he added. "Come, Peale—we'll be right back, father."

"Yes, father, we'll be right back," echoed Peale, as they went out precipitately.

Mr. Martin stood there watching them proudly.

"Bully kid!" he said; then changing to a contemptuous tone: "Ellery Clark!"

Well, that was a load off his mind, at any rate, he reflected contentedly. Of course he had bought a pig in a poke, more or less; you couldn't tell whether their books were carefully audited or not. If Mary Grayson kept them they were probably pretty straight. He was glad to have the boy back again anyway. That was the truth. And there would be no more sandwich men parades.

Altogether he was in a quite mellow mood when Mary Grayson opened the door and came in, looking as sweet as ever, he thought. From the look on her face she was glad to see him, and extraordinarily relieved too. Alas, for the soap king! He did not realize how short his satisfaction was to be.

"Why, Mr. Martin," cried Mary happily.

"Hello, Miss Grayson," he said, "it's mighty good to see you again."

"Oh, Mr. Martin," responded Mary, "I'm so glad Rodney finally sent for you."

"Sent for me?" repeated Mr. Martin in surprise.

"Have you talked to him?" Mary asked.

"Oh yes, he's just gone out for a minute to see the agent of the landlord."

"Oh, then he told you about that too?"

"Yes, he told me — why not?" asked Mr. Martin, puzzled.

"Oh, I'm so glad you've settled with him. You have settled, haven't you?"

"Yes, sure."

"Oh, good. Isn't it wonderful for him?"

The relief in Mary's voice was genuine; — absolutely, as Ambrose Peale would have said. Poor Mary had had a trying day. There had been that dreadful man McChesney, to begin with. Rodney's twenty-five hundred dollar check must have gone through the clearing house in double quick time, Mary had thought, as the advertising dun appeared again. The fact was, it seemed that he had gone to the bank to get it certified, and was furious to find that there were no funds there of the great 13 Soap Company to meet it with. He roared loudly about the sheriff: unless the check was made good at his office in an hour he would have the sheriff round and sell them out, cover up their billboards and send them all to jail. Mary didn't know much about sheriffs, and they sounded terrifying. She had heard about the law's delay, but the law sounded swift and terrible as interpreted by the irate McChesney. She couldn't laugh about it and chaff about a cell with a sunny exposure, as Ambrose Peale did. That awful Countess too! A woman swindler, who had tried to get into them for five thousand dollars. And the Edison man threatening to turn off the light from all their beautiful signs if he wasn't paid at once. How unreasonable people were! How could you pay them when you hadn't any money? And now, last of all, the rent agent making a fuss. No wonder Mary had begged Rodney to send for his father and give in. She did want him to succeed, she told him, but there was no use fighting odds like these. He hadn't any money. He was awfully in debt. He mustn't be disgraced publicly. She was sure old Mr. Martin would help Rodney if he was sent for. Rodney had seemed to waver, and Peale too, even the dauntless Ambrose. Very naturally Mary thought, on seeing Cyrus Martin smoking his cigar there contentedly that he had come in answer to Rodney's summons. She went on, sighing:

"Just think, without you he couldn't have lasted out the day."

"Couldn't what?" ejaculated the astonished soap king; then recovering himself swiftly he added, "Quite so, quite so. Oh, by the way, in our negotiations the one thing Rodney didn't go into fully was the nature of the assets."

"The assets!" laughed Mary gayly. "They

must have amused you. Why, we haven't any."

"Ha, ha! Haven't any?" echoed Mr. Martin, trying to laugh with her.

"But everything's all right now," went on Mary sweetly.

"Oh, yes; great, great," said Mr. Martin; "by the way, there was a report on the street today that the Ivory Soap people were going to make a deal with Rodney — build him a factory —"

"Oh, there's nothing in that," said Mary innocently.

"Are you sure? As I got here I thought I saw Ellery Clark."

"Oh, that wasn't business; he just came to try to borrow some money from Rodney. Wasn't that funny?"

"Oh, yes, very funny," said Martin; then, changing his whole manner, he added angrily:

"The young scoundrel!"

"What!" said Mary.

"Thank you, Miss Grayson, for telling me," said Mr. Martin. "Do you know what he tried to do to me? Hold me up for a hundred thousand dollars, and but for you he'd have succeeded."

"Oh, what have I done?" cried Mary in distress.

"You've saved me a lot of money and kept me from being a fool. That's what you've done. Thank you. Good morning."

"You mean at last he had succeeded in getting you to back him?" cried Mary.

"At last! So that was his scheme all the time — was it? He didn't go into business on the level, but just for my benefit? And you were helping him. Well, he can thank you again for having failed."

"It's all my fault," cried Mary, breaking down.

"Yes, it was from the start. You got up the plan of my pretending to put him out of the house — a mighty silly idea."

"Oh, but I tell you, you must help him," pleaded Mary.

"Help him yourself. You've got five thousand dollars."

"But I gave it to him," cried Mary.

"My son took money from you!"

"He didn't know — I pretended it was from a friend. It made him awfully jealous too," blubbered Mary.

"Well, you got him in — now you can get him out," declared the soap king.

"But your bet," asked Mary! "you bet thirty thousand with John Clark. You don't want to lose that, do you?"

"Well, if Ellery's trying to borrow money from Rodney it looks like an even break. And anyhow I'd lose the bet twice over rather than have my own son think he could make a fool of his father."

"But he is a good business man," pleaded Mary bravely; "he'd make you proud of him. If he could keep on a little longer, I know he'd succeed. If you'll just help him he'll make money, you'll see he will."

"Of course, you want him to make money," said Mr. Martin brutally. "You're thinking of that percentage contract with me."

"I'm not — oh I'm not!" cried Mary. "I can't see him fail. I don't want you to pay me. I'll try to give you back what you've given me. I don't care anything about the contract. I'll tear it up now — if you'll just help him."

Mr. Martin looked at her more leniently.

"By George, I believe you really are in love with him, Mary."

"Yes, I am — now," admitted Mary proudly. "But that doesn't matter. We've got to save him — save his business."

"I won't give him a nickel — good-by!" said Mr. Martin, growing stern again.

"But you can't go like this," Mary cried; "he'll be disgraced — he's in debt — in danger."

"Let him get out of it himself then," said this Roman father. "It'll do him good. I've been a sentimental fool. I've made it all too easy for him."

"But that's your fault too," persisted Mary.

"Yes, it is, and I don't propose to repeat the error; he's lied to me all the way through. We'll let him face the truth now; we'll see what he's made of."

Mary just sat and looked at him quite limply, letting her hands fall idle in her lap. What could she do? To make matters worse she could hear the rumble of men's voices outside as Rodney and Peale tried to soothe the rent agent's righteous indignation. With all her other troubles she must count on this one too. Oh, dear, she thought crossly. She only hoped they would keep on talking till Mr. Martin was gone. But her wish was wasted, for the next minute the outer door swung open and Rodney and Peale came back, trying to look cheerful, but really quite crestfallen, as Mary could see very well.

"Well, we're going to move," said Rodney, going back to his desk.

"Yes, nice chap, that fellow," said Peale.

"Well, Mary, have you heard about our deal?" asked Rodney next.

"The deal's off," Mr. Martin interrupted brusquely.

"But—" began Mary.

"Off?" cried Rodney.

"Off?" echoed Peale.

"Yes, off," repeated Mr. Martin brusquely.

"But why—why?" asked Rodney.

"Because you took me for a bigger fool than I am," said his father. "My own son can't do that to me. I've found out now that you're broke."

"Oh, Mr. Martin," protested Mary, crying.

But Mr. Martin stopped her with a wave of his hand, and went on, addressing Rodney.

"And all the time you were lying to me about the Ivory Soap people and the factory they were going to put up. You thought you could make an ass of me—get the best of me, did you? Well, you can't. I'm finished with you and your 13 Soap. You've got a swelled head, you're a smart Alec, you're a complete fake, you're a cheat, young man—"

"I guess you're right," said Rodney in utter dejection.

"Ah!" said Mr. Martin with some satisfaction.

"I did try to be smart," Rodney said. "I

was stuck on myself. I thought business was a cinch. But you're right. I have been a fake. This whole thing never seemed real — it was just fun — like a game — but I've waked up, and now it's serious. I tried to get the best of you, but I'll take my licking. I don't want any charity. I know what's coming to me, and I'll take my medicine."

His father looked him over curiously.

"Well, maybe I've said a little too much," he said, relenting a little.

"No, it's all true," said Rodney.

"But see here, I don't want you disgraced," said his father. "I —"

"You told me never to come back to you for a nickel," said Rodney bravely, "and I won't. I told you too that I wouldn't snivel. Well, I'm not going to. Good-by, father."

"Now see here," began Martin.

"Please, father," Rodney went on; "it's up to me, and nobody else, to get out of this. Please go."

He held out his hand and Mr. Martin shook it.

"Good-by, son —" he said gently, and went out. His head was bent but he did not look back once.

"Oh, Rodney, Rodney," cried Mary, when the office door had closed on the old man's back.

"Good-by son," he said gently.

"What have I done? And I wanted to help you so."

"Never mind, Mary dear," said the young business man; "you couldn't help it. If you love me everything's all right."

Mary did love him now, she knew. Pity is akin to love, and she pitied the boy, but was proud of him, as she saw him courageously meeting his defeat. She came over to him and kissed him. It was the first time she had ever given him one of her own accord. Rodney hugged her greedily in his arms, before everybody, while Miss Burke coughed and Ambrose Peale blew his nose loudly.

CHAPTER XI

THE TURNING OF THE TIDE

CHAPTER XI

THE TURNING OF THE TIDE

IT was a sad and chastened little company that met in the office next morning. Peale was cast down for once in his life. Mary was pensive, and only Rodney knew that inner glow that gives the silver lining to the cloud of ill luck and poverty. Mary had kissed him: he must put that in his book of days. He thought of her going home in the elevated train, alone that night, because he had had an earlier appointment up town. Usually he took the subway, but to-night he could not bear to think of burying his sacred memory of that kiss beneath the ground: he wanted to be up in the air, to see far away over roofs to the sunset skies. Besides, old Peale took the subway with him every night, and on this special night Rodney wanted to be by himself. He made some excuse and sneaked down Rector Street as best he could alone. He thought of Mary all the way up to his rooms, which were very different ones indeed from his suite in his father's house. He thought of her kiss all night, and sweet Mary, his lode star and saving grace, was uppermost in his mind when he arrived at the office and met her dear self there next morning.

Mary looked at him anxiously and seemed relieved to find him not entirely cast down. She had been wretched herself, she said, worrying over the betrayal of her lover to the old soap king, and began again to bemoan her bad break.

"Oh, Rodney, Rodney," she said to him, "it was all my fault. Your father had no idea of the truth — I didn't understand.— I told him about our company — I did it all — betrayed you."

"But you didn't mean to; it's all right, Mary," said Rodney, reassuring her.

"You forgive me?" asked Mary, looking him in the eyes.

"Why, of course — I love you," he said simply.

"Oh, Rodney, I'm so sorry," Mary began again.

"You're forgiven if you give me another kiss — there," he said; then suddenly changed his tone:

"But if father thinks just because he laced into me I'm licked, he's all wrong," he declared stoutly. "Maybe I have been a fake, but by George, I won't be any longer."

"You're really going on?" Mary asked.

"When I've got you, you bet I am," declared

Rodney. "Do you really think a long speech from father and no money to work with are enough to stop me? No, sir. What father said got me for a minute, but I'm not a quitter, and I'll prove it. I'll get out of this mess the best way I can, and then I'll shine shoes or sell peanuts. I'll start at the bottom instead of finishing there. I'll make money — I'll —"

"Oh, Rodney, Rodney, now I am proud of you," Mary interrupted.

Good old Ambrose Peale had been most sympathetic that morning too. He came up to the little boss, as he had taken to calling Rodney, and put his hand on his shoulder.

"Now see here, little boss," he began.

"Peale, I'm sorry," said Rodney, "but you're fired."

"Oh, no, little boss," said Peale, "you can't fire me. I'm just going to stick around, whatever happens."

Ambrose stuck. In fact, they all stuck. They decided to pay the balance of the month's rent out of their assets, and gave a note to McChesney, to stave him off, as Peale said. Mary protested that a note was money: that it had to be paid some time, but Peale declared that time was money too, and something was sure to happen in the next thirty or sixty days. He felt it in his bones. He pegged away at his advertising meanwhile; it was his dissipation, the liquor in which he drowned his woes. It was his turn whenever any advertising copy began to go out, and he prepared a great deal too that never saw the light of day — by way of practice, he said. His desk fairly bristled with wire hooks and spikes, on all of which the copy and proofs of his ads were thick as a ballet dancer's ruffles. Some of the choicest of these he would exhibit to a caller now and then, and it is even of record that one specially clever stunt was instrumental in getting the redoubtable McChesney to accept the 13 Soap Company's note.

He had books on the science of advertising too, spread on his desk, and may or may not have read them all. Mary's private opinion was that he had not, but that he only drew moral comfort from the outsides of them. At any rate it was astonishing to see how many there were.

"Cheer Up, and Seven Other Things," by Bates, was the title of one of them. Another was "Farrington's Retail Advertising," and then there were Sawyer's "Secrets of the Mail Order Trade," Scott's "Theory of Advertising," Martin's "Commercial Value of Advertising Gratis" — there were dozens of them. There was even one written by a college professor from Missouri.

One favorite little book of Peale's was "The Ginger Cure." Great title that, Peale maintained. Ginger was a business panacea, in the estimation of Ambrose. Most everybody needed ginger, he allowed. It was positively pathetic, Mary thought, sometimes, to see him poring over this "literature," or sitting there scribbling his ads, when the business of shining shoes, which Rodney had threatened to adopt, would have produced more real money for him.

It was the irony of fate that old Cyrus Martin's five thousand dollars, meant to keep carking care from Mary's shoulders, should have been spent in two days on advertising by Ambrose Peale. The explanation of this five thousand dollars must be made to Rodney some day too. Every once in a while he grew curious about it. But Ambrose didn't measure it in dollars and cents, only in terms of space, and still less did he care where it came from. Truly he was a fiend on copy. He would study and expound the signs which they could see from the offiee windows, while Mary, Rodney and Miss Burke would all listen spellbound when there were no callers, as often happened. Not enough white space, he would cry of one emblazonment. Not big enough, he would say. Doesn't bring out the right point, was another criticism. Ain't clear — not true — no punch, et cetera, et cetera.

If only they had just made soap, Mary couldn't help thinking sometimes, as all this talk rang in her ears. If only they had just made soap, and made it good. Good wine needs no bush, was an ancient proverb she came to believe in. By the same token good soap would need no ads.

Now the funniest part of the whole thing, speaking of advertising, was that the 13 Soap, the old family cookbook soap, was really good. Mary had always been loyal to it, from the first time she had used it. She had given it to some friends for Christmas, and they had liked it, too, and said they would "talk it up." She had gone to Dennison's and bought a holly-covered box, and laid three cakes in it, neatly done up in tissue paper and red ribbon, with a stamp showing Santa Claus and a legend, "Not to be opened till Christmas," on the outside.

"We must spell Christmas with an X this year," said Rodney chaffingly. "Let X equal the unknown quantity."

"We'll see," said Mary, smiling.

She simply must go on hoping and smiling or she should die. It was counting your chickens before they were hatched, no doubt, but then you might never get a chance to count them later, she told herself pathetically. She had superintended the first experiments at soap-making and figured out the manufacturing costs. They must be ready, she had always maintained. She even bought a book on elementary chemistry and had dreams of a large soap works, like old Mr. Martin's, where an army of self-supporting girls should be put to work under the best hygienic and sanitary conditions and the minimum wage should be a generous one. She did succeed in getting a few gross of 13 Soap made, after the old Earle formula. In the loft there were a few piles of it, the genuine 13, ranged alongside the pink castile in old rose wrappers. As a matter of fact she had had to give up manufacturing on any large scale, because their advertising took all their money, but Mary cherished the idea of taking up the work in earnest some day again. She didn't really believe much in the idea of making old Mr. Martin buy them out. Already she had more ambitious designs than that for her man Rodney.

Ambrose Peale, the advertising expert, was cynical enough to maintain it did not matter. First create your demand, he would say, then make your soap. Look at the history of the Ingersoll watch people. It took six months to get any returns from advertising any way. In the end, for lack of funds, he carried the day, and Mary, being a wise virgin in her own day, said little. In truth the orders were very, very few. The whole question was the old one of which came first, the chicken or the egg. Their cakes of soap were the eggs and their advertising was the mother chicken that was to hatch out the plentiful brood, if you put it that way; but it was all too metaphysical for Mary, who felt somehow that metaphysics wouldn't help her much with 13 Soap.

This question settled, or rather left *in statu quo*, the soap company's days were all more or less alike. If one omits such visits as those from the Countess, Ellery Clark, and Mr. Martin, who certainly did not drop in frequently, one day was as typical as another. But there came a certain Friday at last which was to finish up in an unusual manner.

The darkest hour comes just before the dawn, and dawn came with a sudden burst of glory one morning when Ambrose Peale flew into the office in great excitement, interrupting Mary and Rodney in a long embrace. Always discreet and tactful, he coughed and scraped his feet, as a signal to them to break away.

"Say, I didn't mean to interrupt," he apologized.

Rodney kept his arms around Mary.

"Nothing in the world can interrupt us," he said. "What is it?"

"A telegram," said Peale, "it's the first we've ever had — I was afraid to open it."

Mary came over to him and looked at it nervously.

"What awful thing can it be?" she queried.

"Gee, I wonder what it says," came from Rodney.

"Read it — read it —" said Peale, afraid to do so himself.

So then Mary opened it and read:

"Rodney Martin, President 13 Soap Company, 339 Broadway —"

"Go on, we know the address," Peale broke in impatiently.

Mary went on:

"Ship at once, collect, fifty thousand cakes 13 Soap.

"Signed: Marshall Field, Chicago."

A profound silence fell upon the trio: the colossal number of fifty thousand, and the magic name of Marshall Field had overpowered them. It was far too good to be true.

"Somebody really wants to buy some of our soap," echoed Rodney stupidly.

"I don't believe it," said Peale.

"But here it is," said Mary, handing the telegram to Rodney, so that he might view it with his own eyes at close range.

"Fifty thousand cakes," said Rodney; "it's true."

Then Peale burst out joyfully; the tide had turned.

"We've started — we've begun!" he yelled; "we're actually going to sell some soap."

"The tide's turned," said Rodney; "didn't I tell you advertising pays? We'll sweep the country — Europe — Asia — Africa. Go in with father? Not for a million dollars!"

"I'll wire Marshall Field right away," said Peale briskly.

"Go ahead, do," said Rodney.

But an exclamation from Mary made them both turn.

"What is it?" asked Peale nervously.

"What's happened?" asked Rodney.

"That order is no good," Mary said sadly.

"What!"

"Why?"

"We can't fill it — we've never made any soap," said Mary with a sinking heart.

"A telegram—I was afraid to open it."

They stood staring at each other aghast.

"What shall we do?" quavered Rodney.

"Let's think," said Peale hopefully.

They sat staring straight ahead dolefully, till finally Rodney remarked slowly:

"We must get some soap."

"Yes, I thought of that," said Peale.

"Where can we get it?" Mary asked them deliberately.

"From a soap factory!" Peale suggested.

"But they all belong to your father," Mary reminded him.

Meanwhile Rodney had a ray of dawning hope.

"But he can't know about this Marshall Field order — maybe we could buy some soap before he'd have a chance to stop them selling to us —"

"Great idea — let's get busy," said Peale, taking him up promptly.

"How?" asked Mary.

"Where's the phone book?" Rodney asked, and grabbed the red classified directory from his desk.

"We'll call up two or three of his branch offiees."

He hurriedly began turning over pages, as Peale on one side and Mary on the other helped him.

"Skins, skates, shirts, where's soap?" he recited.

"Skylights, slates, slides —" echoed Mary over his shoulder.

"Smelters, smokestacks, snuff," went on Peale.

"Ah, here it is, soap manufacturers," said Rodney at last, skimming down the page. "276 Broad — here's one of father's factories."

"I've got one too — 374 Schuyler," said Peale.

"So have I — 480 Audubon," Mary chimed in.

With one accord they dropped the book and darted to the telephones, shouting all together:

"276 Broad."

"480 Audubon."

"374 Schuyler, and hurry, sweetie —"

"It'll have to be old rose," said Rodney in an aside, as he held the wire.

"Castile is the cheapest," Peale suggested.

"Order small cakes," said the prudent Mary. And then they all began again together:

"Hello, is this the Martin Soap Company? We want to get some soap — pink castile — small cakes — forty or fifty thousand cakes — immediate delivery — what's the price?" . . .

"Hello 480 Audubon. I want to find out if I can buy a lot of soap right away — old rose —

castile — fifty thousand cakes, we want it this afternoon. . . ."

"Hello — son, I want to buy a lot of soap, fifty thousand cakes; got to have some of it to-day — smallest size castile cakes you keep — if you haven't old rose — pink'll do.— Who am I? None of your business." . . .

This last message, with its bit of airy persiflage, came from Peale, who looked at the others and gave a large and happy wink as he surveyed them waiting at their receivers.

The tide had turned.

CHAPTER XII

SOAP BUBBLES

CHAPTER XII

SOAP BUBBLES

THEY could hardly wait till the soap came in and was shipped out again to Chicago. All three of them were as excited as children waiting before the doors that open on a Christmas tree. Fifty thousand cakes! It was an inestimable, an infinite, an incredible, number. Rodney had not an idea whether a row of fifty thousand cakes of 13 Soap would reach from our earth to the moon, or only from the Plaza to the Pennsylvania Terminal. They came and came, an endless chain. But when the influx stopped and had been carefully counted by Mary, Miss Burke and the office boy, pro tem., it totaled, not fifty thousand, though it seemed a million, but only five thousand altogether.

"Are you sure?" asked Peale and Rodney in one breath. "Aren't there any more?"

"Quite sure," said Mary.

"Positive," said Miss Burke.

"Are you certain sure there aren't any more of them anywhere?" repeated Ambrose.

"Search me," said the office boy.

It was true; only five thousand of the lot had been delivered.

The company's three officers made a dash for their telephones. Peale got 374 Schuyler, Mary 480 Audubon and Rodney 276 Broad in a jiffy, only to be told that there was no more soap in stock. In each instance the news was conveyed in a cool and uncordial tone that gave them to understand there was nothing more doing in that quarter. What was the matter?

Peale turned round and stared at his companions and partners aghast.

"Well, wouldn't that get you?" he ejaculated.

Rodney was the most crestfallen of them all, for an idea had come to him of the true reason of things.

"It's the pater," he said in a quiet tone that carried conviction. "He's shut down on us."

Mary set her lips and nodded her head in her turn, for the same idea had occurred to her. She was afraid it was all too true. As one sometimes even in a nightmare tells oneself this horrible sensation is a dream, so she told herself now this cruel, horrible refusal to give them more soap was only a part of old Mr. Martin's bluff to make Rodney work, one more of his "Scenes" in his grand scheme to transform Rodney from an idle rich man's son into a real money getter; that to-morrow, in real life, the other cakes would come.

In one mental flash she would see the thing this way and now that. She liked old Mr. Martin. He had been kind to her in many ways, and even in that one special sentimental way which made Mary feel that she wielded an influence over him. She knew her mother's story — women are seldom perfectly silent as to the men that love them — and she would not believe he could turn her loose. And yet he had been angry, really angry, about those sandwich men and the false statement. Oh, dear, oh, dear! How hard it was to run straight in business and make money.

Then she began to look on the more practical side of things, to turn round and see where they stood. An order for five thousand cakes in itself was not so bad. It was the very largest they had ever received, at any rate; they would ship the five thousand promptly and Marshall Field would pay cash for them in ten days. She made a rapid calculation. They were giving old Mr. Martin three cents a cake for them, and would get three thousand dollars back. That would mean two thousand eight hundred and fifty dollars. She smoothed out the frown in her pretty forehead and announced aloud:

"Well, it means about three thousand to us, and cash too. After all that's not so bad."

Peale cheered up immediately.

"Cash," he repeated, rolling the word round in his mouth and tasting it. "The most beautiful word in the English language."

"Except one," said Rodney, looking at Mary.

"Which is?" Peale queried.

"Love," said Rodney.

"No, cash," said Peale. "Why, look here; think what this means, three thousand dollars."

"We'll discount McChesney's note," said Mary resolutely.

"And it's only a beginning," went on Peale. "Give me back that telegram. It'll be my letter of credit, my passport and all the rest of it? I'll show it to the advertising agents. They'll trust me on the strength of that."

It proved a help indeed, this cash, when it came on in due course, but not a cure. It vanished like smoke in thin air, like cream before a set of kittens, like snow upon the desert's dusty face. Their joy in it was short lived, because it was so soon gone. Again there came a day when the end of the month, with its next rent payment, seemed much nearer than the first; a day when time, which Peale said was the same thing as money, seemed very much like time, and short time at that, and very little like real money. To make matters worse Peale meanwhile had swung round the circle again, waving his "letter of credit," and running up a lot more in the way of bills on new advertising. He had scooted off for a week and never let the office know by so much as a telegram where he was. Then, as cheerfully as he had gone, he blew home again one day announcing that he had contracted for about thirty thousand dollars' worth of advertising in Boston, Baltimore, Philadelphia, Washington and a few other eastern metropolises. He declared it was the greatest advertising campaign ever undertaken since George W. Advertising was a young man. Just look at some of this copy, he told Mary, flourishing a bunch of proofs. When she took him to task for not keeping in touch with the home office he said he had done it on purpose, my dear; he wanted to make a splendid entrance. Really he was hopeless, thought poor Mary.

For a self-respecting bookkeeper it was all dreadfully disheartening; Mary sighed and found it very difficult. Making five go into two was nothing compared with the effort to make twenty-two thousand eight hundred and eighteen dollars and nine cents go into one hundred and thirty-three dollars and thirteen cents. Mary remembered the story of the millionaire socialist who wouldn't separate himself from his money and divide it up with the poor because there would be so little for each poor man when he got his share. Such would certainly be the case with their creditors if she attempted to make their assets go any distance at all. Oh dear, oh dear! How discouraging it all was. She couldn't help repining, once in a while, for the old comfortable days when she had just drawn her money regularly each week, and hadn't expected much in the way of riches, and hadn't set her mind on stirring up the idle rich. How far away that afternoon in Mr. Martin's library seemed now! In her mind's eye that minute she could see Rodney as he came in the front door downstairs with the big white carnation in his buttonhole.

For a little while the days passed uneventfully, drawing nearer the inevitable end. Then came the last day of the month, and Mary's blue devils were very large and blue. The day passed quietly enough in the 13 Soap Company's offices, so far as outward signs revealed it; there were few callers, McChesney being out of the way, though Mary knew he would be heard from to-morrow if his note was not properly met at the bank. How was she ever going to get a check certified to meet it!

Rodney at his desk sat quietly absorbed. He

rustled a few papers now and then, and used his rubber stamp, but its impact on the pad and paper lacked the usual vigor. Even Peale's head, Mary noted, drooped a little as he wrote his ads — ads that would be born to blush unseen if money could not be raised somehow, somewhere, to pay for them. The truth was that for once in their business life all three of them, president, secretary and advertising agent, usually so keen on business, sat there like schoolboys with their eyes upon the clock, waiting for the hour to close.

As the hour of five drew near Mary began to make some long drawn out preparations for going home. This last quarter of an hour of time must be killed and done to death by fair means or by foul. A resolution had been slowly forming in her head, and now took definite shape. She shut down her desk with a delightfully loud noise, and stood up.

"I may be a little late to-morrow," she said to Rodney, as she began putting on her hat.

"All right," said the president mildly.

Rodney too looked as if something were working in his mind, and no wonder, Mary thought, with their situation what it was. Mary knew him like a book, but this time she would ask no questions and keep her own counsel. She was going straight up to Mr. Martin's on Fifth Avenue and have a long talk and argument with him. He simply *must* let them have those extra forty-five thousand cakes of soap for Marshall Field.

She scurried over to the Third Avenue elevated and climbed the stairs of the station at Worth Street, her brain working all the time. In a curious, detached spirit she saw her nickel slide into the groove made by so many previous nickels on the hard wood sill under the office window, and dropped her ticket delicately in the ticket chopper's glass box. A local train was what she wanted, because she was more likely to get a seat there and have a chance to think, so she strolled up and down a moment and then sat down on one of the green seats on the plaform. It was nice to get the fresh air and rest a moment, though the signs that stared at her across the track reminded her of Ambrose and their business escapades. How many advertisements there were, and how much money was being spent on them, if half what Ambrose said was true! What a character Ambrose was! What he said must be true too, and there actually were results, sometimes. There was the Marshall Field order to prove it. If only Mr. Martin could be wheedled into selling them that extra soap!

Several local trains passed, all crowded, and, being tired, and enjoying the fresh air, Mary was disposed to take her time and wait till she got the seat she wanted. It gave her a luxurious feeling to let the trains go by and not run after them, as people usually did in New York.

A woman came presently and sat down beside her, with an evident inclination to talk. She was young, though her peroxide hair made her look older. There were two types of women with dyed hair like this, Mary had noted — the fast and the sentimental. Her neighbor was obviously the latter, and Mary's looks had probably appealed to her. Without insolence she looked Mary over thoroughly a moment as if appraising her.

"Are you a business woman?" she asked after a little pause.

Mary was good-natured and a good mixer, and, seeing that the woman suffered only from human curiosity, she answered, "Yes," adding just for fun:

"I'm a vice-president and a secretary. Our company has offices on Broadway."

The woman looked quite impressed.

"What line are you folks in?" she pursued.

"Soap," said Mary.

"Married?" asked the woman.

"Not yet," said Mary.

"Well, you'll get a husband, if you want one," said the woman with a crisp laugh. "A pretty girl like you usually gets what's coming to her."

"I'm engaged," said Mary, amused.

"You see?" said the woman. "Now I'm a bachelor maid, as they call them nowadays, myself. Most of my girl friends have too much trouble with their husbands. None of your married life for mine. No, sir. No matter how swell a little home I might have, it wouldn't appeal to me!"

Mary laughed at this cynicism.

"When are you going to be married?" the woman inquired, still chatty and curious.

"Oh, I don't know," said Mary. "I suppose we'll go down to the city hall some day and have it over with."

"You'd like a nice wedding though, wouldn't you?" the woman continued sympathetically; "with white satin and a wedding veil and all. I know one girl who's never got over it because she was married in a brown dress."

Mary was used to these unreticent interlocutors, going about the crowded city as she did. The woman with the dyed hair rushed off presently, shrieking, "Oh, there's Mayme," and she was left alone again. The local that she waited for, originating further up town than South Ferry, came along and she got aboard at her leisure.

She had a choice of seats, in fact, and took one on the left side in one of the middle compartments, so she could see the broad Bowery as she passed through it. The traffic of the street flashed by like a moving picture as she rode on — past Saint Gaudens's Peter Cooper in his bronze armchair near Bible House, past Fourteenth Street and Tammany Hall, on through the twenties and thirties and under the Forty-second Street shuttle train, over Sixtieth Street with its stream of motors from the Queensboro Bridge, and on up to the Seventy-second Street station. Through this broad lane Mary trudged bravely west, keeping her courage at the striking point, and pressed the bell button on Mr. Cyrus Martin's front door. Johnson, looking surprised but pleased to see her, let her in, and showed her into the little reception room downstairs to wait, while he took her name up to Mr. Martin.

A host of memories trooped round her as she sat on the gilt sofa. The quiet and comfort of the big house soothed her nerves in spite of herself, but she felt a pang too, to think of all Rodney had turned his back on. How perverse it was of fate to give all this to old men who couldn't really enjoy it and deny it to young people who could taste and relish it to the full. The reflection challenged her. She was going to do whatever she could to bring Rodney's father round before the iron entered too deeply into the boy's soul. She cared more for him now than for riches or success or advertising or anything at all.

There had been a curious pleasure in telling that perfect stranger just now about her engagement, and talking about being married.

Sitting in the little room she couldn't help reviewing the course of her life for the last six months. First there was her coming up to this fine house here, at the old gentleman's insistence, and her first seeing Rodney, a being unlike any other male she had known till then. Then there was old Mr. Martin's scheme to have the boy go to work. Mr. Martin had tried to make out that she, Mary, had conceived the idea of waking Rodney up, that she had invented the paternal gout, etc. Had she? —

And then Ambrose Peale and the 13 Soap Company and their joyous new adventuring into the deep sea of business; their troubles and their worries, and Rodney's pluck in sticking at it — She recalled it all in quick flashes of thought. Should she give in herself now —" quit"? Never —

" Mr. Martin will see you, Miss Grayson," said Johnson, coming back; and she followed him upstairs with beating heart.

CHAPTER XIII

SOAPSUDS

CHAPTER XIII

SOAPSUDS

IF there is any time in the day when a retired business man should be allowed to enjoy himself in his own mature and self chosen way, it is the hour between five and six. This hour "between the dark and the daylight" was not the children's hour in Mr. Martin's house, for good and sufficient reasons, his only son having been cast off and there being no "grands" yet anyway. Neither was it a five o'clock tea hour, for Mr. Martin never had tea any more since Mary Grayson had gone: he had had Johnson bring it in for her once in a while in the old days, to feed her up, but not now. His new secretary was a goose, and he had packed her off, and now he found some letters to open with his own hands to-day, which seemed to annoy him. Disgruntlement still swayed his paternal heart when he thought of Rodney — he was torn between love and irritation where that boy was concerned.

He turned to the papers for consolation and held one sheet up to scrutinize the headlines. As he did so he displayed to the empty room a full page adventisement of 13 Soap — the hand of Ambrose, in fact — which by some occult influence presently impelled him to turn the paper over and glance at the last page next. The blatant sprawling ad caused him a pang of regret and disgust, and he flung it down. He took up another paper and had the same experience, then turned angrily to some letters, only to be rewarded by the sight of 13 Soap circulars fluttering to the floor when he opened the envelope — the hand of Ambrose again in fact. Another "letter" and another — they had got a beastly way now of addressing them in refined female hands, on good stationery, so you'd think they were invitations — followed the first into the waste paper basket.

It was a relief when Johnson presently appeared and announced a caller, though a great surprise to hear the caller's name. Mary Grayson! Now what was this sly puss after? he speculated as he bade Johnson show her in. Come to get her old job back, he supposed. Well, she could have it, at her old salary. He said this last aloud to her, as she came into the room looking very sweet, he must admit. The serious expression she wore was not at all unbecoming to her pretty face.

The room looked just as it used to do, and the recollection took Mary back again, in spite of her engrossing errand. The diamond pendulum was still swinging on the mantelpiece. Mr. Martin himself wound all the clocks in the house every Sunday morning, at exactly half-past nine, when the hands did not interfere with the key holes.

"But I don't want it," said Mary, in response to his ungracious proposition.

"Oh, then, Rodney has sent you to plead for him," suggested Mr. Martin.

"No, sir," said Mary. "He doesn't know I'm here."

"Then what are you here for?" he demanded, really curious.

"To make you a business proposition," said Mary stoutly.

"Why doesn't Rodney make it himself?" asked his father.

"He doesn't know what it is," explained Mary.

"That's something in his favor," Martin conceded; "I can't see much use in women tying up in men's business. Somehow I love the scallawag, and, damn it, I miss him around here."

He looked at Mary curiously as he said this, wondering how she and Rodney were getting along these days and what her errand really was, though he didn't propose to give away his interest in it. She had betrayed the true nature of things to him once. What was she going to do now?

His reflections and Mary's business were interrupted, however, by Johnson's entering a second time and announcing the last two people in the world that Mary had counted on, namely, Mr. Rodney Martin and Mr. Ambrose Peale.

"Oh, the whole firm, eh?" said Mr. Martin, eyeing Mary sharply.

Mary started guiltily. For a moment she feared that Rodney might hark back to that five thousand dollar check his father had given her and grow jealous again. She couldn't pretend to be pleased to see him, despite her sentimental reflections just now downstairs. She had wanted to handle this interview in her own way. She felt she could have done it right, convincingly, just as a hunter feels within himself that he can clear the hurdle that looms up ahead. Now, here were Rodney and Ambrose to interfere with her, and Ambrose of course would interrupt and switch her off and perhaps irritate the old gentleman with his advertising talk. He couldn't help it. Ambrose would pop out of his jack-in-the-box instanter if you sprung the subject of soap and advertising.

Old Mr. Martin surveyed all three of them grimly, just long enough to let embarrassment set in on all their faces. His eyes rested on Mary last of all, and longest. A fairly perceptible change crept round his firm old mouth as he did so. He was satisfied the little minx had told him the truth about Rodney's not knowing anything as to her mission here, and indeed, when the boy came in and saw her there, he exclaimed in genuine surprise:

"Why, Mary, what are you doing here?"

Mary thought fast a moment, and evidently decided that the best part of diplomacy this time was the truth.

"I came to tell your father about Marshall Field," she said frankly.

Rodney looked relieved.

"That's why we're here too," he said.

"Absolutely," added Peale.

"Well, what is it about Marshall Field?" blustered Martin. "Let me tell you right now, I won't back any fake company."

"But we're not a fake any longer," protested Rodney.

"We've actually sold some soap," chimed in Peale.

"Fifty thousand cakes," Mary explained impressively.

"To Marshall Field," said Rodney.

"Then why did you send 'em only five thousand cakes?" inquired old Martin bluntly.

"Because after we'd got that much from one of your branch factories you shut off our supply."

"And we couldn't get any more soap anywhere," said Peale plaintively.

"And you knew it very well," Mary said accusingly.

"We've still got forty-five thousand cakes to deliver, if we can get 'em from you," went on Rodney; "why let all that money get out of the family?" he pleaded; "it's a business proposition."

"No, it isn't," said his father; "don't fool yourself; I sent that telegram."

"What telegram?" asked Rodney.

"The telegram from Marshall Field's ordering the fifty thousand cakes," grunted old Martin.

Mary plumped down on a chair in dismay.

"You sent it?" she gasped.

Mr. Martin decided to amplify a little.

"That day at the office you were pretty game, son," he said; "and to tell the truth I felt so sorry for you I had to do something; so I sent that wire —"

"So that success is all a bluff too?" sighed Rodney.

"Well," said his father, "I figured an order like that would stall off your creditors, and when

I had fixed it with one of our factories to let you have five thousand cakes at three cents a cake I knew it would mean some ready cash for you from Marshall Field —"

"But how did you square Marshall Field?" inquired Peale, still hoping it was his ads.

"Oh, I just wired 'em I'd be responsible," said Mr. Martin; "and say," he added, turning to Rodney, "you had a nerve to charge 'em sixty cents a cake. I had to pay the bill. That shipment cost me three thousand dollars for one hundred and fifty dollars' worth of soap."

Peale laughed.

"That isn't funny, young man," said Mr. Martin, glaring at him.

"No, it isn't," admitted Rodney. "I thought we'd really made good, and all the time it was you behind us —"

"You see, my boy," said Martin senior, "even if you did nearly trim me, I've got a sort of sneaking fondness for you. Look here, son, why not quit? There's no market for dollar soap."

"But how do you know?" Rodney objected bravely.

"How do I know?" asked his father. "Because I had a letter from Marshall Field a few days ago asking me what to do with the soap.

They hadn't sold a cake. I told 'em to dump it in the Chicago river. It might help the drainage canal."

"But you didn't give our advertising a chance," objected Rodney.

"Yes," said Peale eagerly. "We only finished a great big advertising campaign in Chicago two days ago."

"I know the soap would have made good," insisted Rodney, "with that trademark."

"If your trademark was so marvelous," said Martin, "somebody besides your poor old father would have bought your soap."

In the meantime Peale had grown more and more discouraged.

"Oh, what's the use? He doesn't believe in advertising," he said pathetically.

"Oh yes, I do," Mr. Martin objected; "sound conservative advertising, but not the crazy, sensational stuff you go in for."

Mary decided she would try another tack.

"Oh, you're just mad because the soap trust didn't think of 13 Soap itself," she said, half mischievously.

"Why, we wouldn't touch a fool thing like that," said Mr. Martin. "If you deliver the goods, your goods will advertise you; that's always been our policy."

This was an unfortunate lead for the old soap king to have made. To doubt the efficiency of his ads was to strike at the vitals of Ambrose Peale, to challenge him and draw his fire every time. And now Rodney was his enthusiastic squire and second.

Both boys drew good long breaths and began on their favorite themes. Poor Mary felt that she too was being swept along with them in the flood of Peale's enthusiasm.

"I'm sorry, father," Rodney led off, "but you are too old fashioned to know the modern way of advertising. Why, do you know the National Biscuit Company was on the verge of failing until they hit on the title Uneeda Biscuit?"

Mary took a hand, too.

"And since then, they have had over four hundred law-suits to protect it," quoted Mary.

"Their trademark made 'em," Rodney went on. "They value that trademark now at six million dollars."

Peale had listened with grim satisfaction.

"Great stuff," he echoed, then added:

"And spearmint gum, just as a trademark, is worth seven millions."

"And the Fairbanks people count their trademark, The Gold Dust Twins, at ten millions," said

"And did you ever hear of the Gillette Safety Razor?" asked Mary. "Tell him about it, Rodney."

"It costs you five dollars," said Rodney; "don't you know there's a mighty good safety razor for a quarter and dozens at a dollar? But you use the Gillette because Gillette was there first. You buy his razor at a high price simply because of its trademark."

"Advertising," said Mary, with a gesture she had learned from Rodney.

"Absolutely," said Rodney, with a word he had learned from Peale.

Peale himself went on:

"And Ivory soap in the magazines alone used four hundred and fifty thousand dollars' worth of space in 1913; and at three cents a cake wholesale that represents fifteen million cakes for magazine advertising alone."

"I don't believe it," old Martin interrupted.

"Yes," said Peale irreverently, "and a lot of other guys didn't believe that iron ships would float, or that machines heavier than air would fly, or that you could talk to Chicago on a wire, or send a message across the Atlantic without a wire. Pardon me, sir, but you want to get on to yourself."

"Yes, father, you certainly do," said Rodney.

"And you'd better hurry up," added Mary.

Mr. Martin laughed grimly.

"You've got a fine lot of theories, but what have they done for those five thousand cakes of 13 Soap out at Marshall Field's?"

"Why, we haven't really spent enough money advertising," said Peale, true to his faith. "That's the trouble."

"That's true," Rodney agreed. "Every time the American Tobacco Company puts out a new cigarette they start off by appropriating two hundred thousand dollars to boom it."

"And I suppose they are a lot of boobs," put in Peale.

"And think what other firms spend," said Rodney. "I've gone into this thing, father —"

"Yes, Rodney, let's show him our list," said Mary.

Rodney and Peale each grabbed a long typewritten sheet out of his breast pocket. Mary too produced a list from her shopping bag, frugally written on an envelope back.

"Sure," Rodney said. "It's an absolutely accurate list of what some of the big advertisers spent in the thirty-one leading magazines last year. Eastman Kodak," he began to read off: "four hundred thousand. Postum Coffee, one hundred and thousand, Philip Morris Cigarettes, one hundred thousand, Welch's Grape Juice, one hundred thousand."

"Grape Juice, my friend," put in Peale, winking.

"Uneeda Biscuit one hundred and fifty thousand, Spearmint Gum one hundred and forty thousand," pursued Rodney.

"That's enough; that's enough," protested his father.

"Oh, I've only just begun," Rodney laughed. "Grape Nuts two hundred and twenty-eight thousand."

"Colgate's Dental Cream, two hundred and thirty thousand," mentioned Mary.

"Campbell's Soups, one hundred and eighty-six thousand," said Peale.

"Kellogg's Toasted Cornflakes, two hundred thousand," said Mary.

"Quaker Oats, three hundred sixty-seven thousand, and these are only a few," said Rodney. "You can't see how it pays, but you do know that it must pay or they wouldn't do it."

"Doesn't all that mean anything to you?" inquired Mary anxiously.

"Yes, doesn't it?" Peale persisted.

"When you realize that those thirty-one magazines have only about ten million readers?" said Mary.

"And that there are a hundred million people in this country?" resumed Rodney. "Why, just to appeal to one-tenth of the population fifty million dollars was spent in magazines last year and each year people are getting better educated — more people are wanting to read. It won't be long before there are twenty-five million people buying magazines, and you can reach all of them by advertising — get a new market, a new population to deal with. Think what national advertising is accomplishing. It sells automobiles, vacuum cleaners, talking machines, rubber heels, kodaks, washing machines, foods, clothes, shoes, paints, houses, plumbing, electric irons, fireless cookers, mostly to a lot of people who'd never even hear of 'em if it weren't for advertisements."

Peale took up the refrain next.

"But nowadays it isn't only people who have stoves to sell or tooth brushes that are spending money on publicity," he began. "Banks are advertising for money, nations for immigrants, colleges for students, cities for citizens and churches for congregations; and you sit there thinking it doesn't pay to advertise."

"Six hundred and sixteen million dollars were

spent last year in magazines and newspapers, bill-boards and electric signs," recited Mary.

"Bringing education and comfort and fun and luxury to the people of the United States," said Rodney. "It's romance, father, the romance of printing presses, of steel rails, of the wireless, of trains and competition, the romance of modern business, and it's all built on advertising. Why, advertising is the biggest thing in this country, and it's only just begun."

Mr. Martin let them pause a while, out of breath.

"Why didn't you boys go into the advertising business?" he asked. "You seem to know something about that."

This was too much for Peale, who began fairly tearing his hair:

"Oh, what's the use? He's the old school. We're new blood."

"Yes, youth has got it on old age," agreed Rodney.

"Indeed, it has," said Mary.

"Well," said Mr. Martin, "when you boys get through talking, and you're flat broke and down and out, come around and see me; I'll show you an old business that has a lot of money, that isn't radical, and that manages to keep going without wasting a fortune in fool advertising."

"Then you won't let us get any soap?" asked Rodney.

"Risk my business reputation on a silly scheme like dollar soap, I should say not. You may be crazy, but I'm not."

"Yes, you are," said Mary, beginning to lose her temper.

"Oh, come on," said Peale impatiently. "What's the use of talking to a man whose brain is deaf?"

The old soap king only laughed.

"Say, when you get a spiel come around," he chaffed. "I like to hear you talk dollar soap."

And so to the accompaniment of his scornful chuckles the three dejectedly walked out. Poor Mary's mission had failed. In the street outside she couldn't help pouting a little, especially for Rodney's benefit, and she scolded Peale outright. She was sure she could have managed the old gentleman if she had been allowed to do it in her own intuitive woman's way, and she told both the boys so flatly. What was the use of spouting all those statistics? What they wanted was forty-five thousand cakes of soap, not five thousand words of advertising talk. What impression had they made on the soap king? Not the slightest.

brose. " Just let it sink in and rankle a bit, and we'll see."

" Nonsense," said Mary quite crossly.

She set out for home on the other side of the park on foot, and declined Rodney's escort peremptorily, hardening her heart. As she left she could hear him and Peale debating whether to spend ten cents on the bus or five on the Madison Avenue cars to get themselves home. Alas, the last time they had left this house together, she and Rodney, it had been a choice between the bus and a taxi.

[illegible] and [illegible] a bit, and

[illegible] quite [illegible].
[illegible] the other side of the
[illegible] Rodney's [illegible] per-
[illegible]. [illegible] the left she
[illegible] whether to
[illegible] on the Madison
[illegible]. Alas, the
[illegible] together, she and
[illegible] between the bus and

CHAPTER XI

AMBROSE PEAI

CHAPTER XIV.

AMBROSE PEALE

AS a matter of fact each went a different route, for Rodney climbed up on a stage to get the fresh air, he said, and Peale wended his way east on foot.

Poor Ambrose! He wouldn't have admitted it to anybody in the world but for once in his life he was downcast and discouraged. His unfailing goodnature was cloaked and veiled a little, and no mistake. He was blue.

What was worse his blues lasted, off and on,

them down town. His companions in the company did not see the drooping of his spirits any more than they guessed the dreary view of New York backyards that he saw from his windows when he reached the place that stood him in the stead of home.

He let himself in the front door of his boarding house, one afternoon late, kicking the pink gas bill that had been tucked beneath it as he crossed the threshold, and his nose was assailed by that familiar but never enjoyable, mingled odor of cats and turnips that pervades the basements of old New York. He ate his dinner grimly and climbed the stairs to his back room, throwing himself into the shabby rocking chair, of the vintage of the early eighties, which constituted the one luxury of his small cubicle. Even the cigar which he presently lighted failed of its usual solace. The caterwauling of some cats and the barking of a dog on the other side of the fence came up to him from the yard below, sustained by the heavy rumble of the Third Avenue elevated. It was the hour when the express trains were bringing their toiling thousands up town from dingy offices to shabby homes. Lucky slaves, he thought, not to know the meaning of those dread words, assets and liabilities. If they hated their bosses they might console themselves with the thought that bosses had sometimes more worries than theirs.

In the distance he could see the long graceful strand of lights on the Queensboro Bridge. The peculiar mournful whistle of the Fall River boat sounded, passing Blackwell's Island as usual at this hour and signaling importantly to other craft. With unaccustomed sensitiveness to these impressions a taste of world-smart struck sharply to the soul of Ambrose Peale. He stood up and yawned and stretched, throwing his cigar into the chipped cuspidor near the washstand. What was the use of it all anyway?—

As the criminal returns to the scene of his crime so Ambrose's spirit was drawn back to his old haunts of the show world again. The Queensboro lights were tiny candles compared with the blaze of Broadway's electric lane. He put on a clean collar, retied his four-in-hand and went out.

Riding down in the red cars through the gaudy glare of Third Avenue and transferring west on Forty-second Street, he fluttered like a moth to the blaze of the Great White Way. Was he tired of the 13 Soap Company? Did his faith in advertising begin to wane? Or did Mary and Rodney, billing and cooing in the office when he came upon them unawares, give him some hint of he liked them both. And he had for Rodney the kind of undemonstrative affection that springs up sometimes between men when they have fought side by side in the battlefield of business. If he thought his being in the company prejudiced the old gentleman against Rodney he would —

"Hello, Mr. Pe-e-ele."

He was interrupted in his altruistic intentions by a shrill feminine voice sounding his name in an accent that blended the Bowery and Berlitz, and turned to see the "Countess." They were in front of the Knickerbocker, and she was headed for the revolving doors on Forty-second Street. Peale gravitated at once to her side and jumped into the whirling compartment behind her.

"Well, cutie," he said, as they dropped down together on a lounge in the crowded corridor, "what are you up to?"

People were passing hither and there, coming from the restaurant and going on to the play. The revolving storm doors swung round continuously, reminding Peale of the scheme he had once conceived of utilizing their power for driving dynamos. Great scheme it was; but nothing ever came of it. Ambrose didn't need dynamos himself to electrify him where a pretty woman like the Countess was concerned.

"You're a grand little guy," said the Countess agreeably; "I like you."

But all the time her eyes roved round the place as if she were looking for another man.

"How are you getting along now?" she went on. "As far as I'm concerned, trim everybody you can. You're there, Ambrose, you're there."

"But we're on the level," Peale assured her.

"So am I," said the Countess.

"If you were I'd give you a job," laughed Peale.

"Me work on a job," cried the Countess; "there's no excitement in that. Why, now every time I meet a cop I get a thrill."

"I know — I know; the dull life is dull," Peale agreed. "I wonder if I ought to marry you and reform you?"

"No, Ambrose," said the Countess quite sincerely; "I wouldn't do such a thing to you as marry you. I could talk to you about your needing a loving faithful wife, and maybe you do at that. But the trouble with me is I'd rather trim a guy out of a hundred than earn a thousand; so leave me lay, kid, leave me lay —"

At this moment, Peale, following her gaze, saw what she was looking for, and apparently "it" paint, was wandering up and down evidently looking for her.

"Shall I bring him over?" asked Peale.

"No," said the Countess; "wait a moment. I want to talk to you a second about Ellery. He's kind of stuck on me," she added shyly.

"Say, I'm for you," broke in Peale, "but if you're aiming to trim Ellery I can't help you there; it'd be too easy."

"Easy! You don't know Ellery — he's wise all right," she protested.

"Funny — I thought you were a smart dame," Peale retorted; "and yet you think Ellery is wise —"

"Well, they say love is blind," said the girl, smiling.

"Say, I don't like Ellery," said Peale quickly, "but if you're planning to Maxixe down the bridal path with him I won't stand for it."

"Oh, I wouldn't hitch up. No, Ambrose, you got me wrong," said the Countess plaintively.

"What is the graft, then?"

The Countess looked at him with a great show of dignity.

"Say, Mr. Peale," she said, "don't you think I got some sense of decency? And anyhow, I wouldn't go after Ellery. He'd be on in a minute. No, sir, I stack up against men of my own size; ducks who think they're wise guys, like you and your young partner."

"Well, what is the idea with Ellery then?" Peale asked uncomfortably.

"You may not like him," the Countess began; "he does seem kind of a stuck up nut; but when you get to know him he's a nice kid — He's got a car, he loves to go to shows, he slips the headwaiter five, says, 'Bring us a good dinner and two bottles of 149; — he can sign checks anywhere; he's a grand little companion for a lonely dame like me. He looks forward to seeing me. He phones me every morning and just sticks around. He don't even try to hold my hand."

"Well, where do I come in?" Peale insisted.

"You're going to see him now," the Countess said; "just don't slip it to him I'm a grafter, will you? It'd bust up the whole thing — I'll play straight with him — just pals. You don't know how hard it is for girls like me. I never had a show — I ran away from home when I was a kid. I've been pretty up against it sometimes, and now this boy comes along and treats me fine. Is what I've done to other guys to butt in and queer me? Oh, Ambrose, don't bowl me out with Ellery."

"Nix, nix," said Peale, pulling out his handkerchief.

on the Countess. "It ain't easy for a girl to fight it out just by herself, when she's all alone; no money, no friends and she's got to live — live on five a week in a back room lookin' out on a brick wall, and cook over the gas. Food and clothes and live on five per —! You got a lot for a good time — haven't you? That's what I had to do. God, I was lonely sometimes. You've got to be pretty smart to steer straight. But I've done it — I've done it!"

With that she broke down and began to snivel.

"Now, see here, Countess," said Peale kindly, patting her on the back. "Don't do that — don't, don't —" Then after a pause he added:

"Oh, quit it — keep it for some poor boob who'll fall for it."

"Oh, Ambrose — don't talk like that," said the Countess tearfully.

"Say, honest, it's foolish wasting it on me — kid," said Peale.

"Well, it's always worth trying once," said the girl, completely changing to a radiant smile.

"Sure it is," said Peale genially. "Why, you had me winging for a minute. But when you pulled that five a week gag — and the ancient wheeze about steering straight, I knew it was the antique phoney stuff."

"I learned it from a play — great, isn't it?

It always goes. But at that I'm on the level about Ellery. I just couldn't keep from drifting into dramatics. Do tell him I'm a real French dame."

"Absolutely," said Peale. "Hello, Peter Piccadilly," he added, as Ellery at last discovered them; "what brings you to the haunts of pleasure?"

He didn't wait for Ellery's answer, but promptly vacated the place at the girl's side and left them to each other and their fates.

In his present mood the meeting and the talk for all his chaff, only strengthened the wings of his black butterflies. The sight of Ellery Clark completed his distaste with the whole sorry scheme of things, making him itch to remold it nearer to his heart's desire. Ellery Clark, that pinhead, went round with girls who trimmed him like the "Countess," supplied with plenty of money by his doting father, while Rodney and Mary had to slave and worry.

It was all wrong, unnatural. Something must be the matter between old Rodney and his father, and he believed he knew what it was. He would go up and see old Mr. Martin at once, to-night, before it was too late. No, not to-night, to-morrow morning, Saturday, when the soap mag-

Saturday afternoon, after lunch, when people were more apt to feel gay and good-natured.

That was how, as a consequence of this mood and various meetings and reflections, Ambrose Peale came to give his name to Johnson at the soap king's house next day.

CHAPTER XV

A DEAL

CHAPTER XVI

A DEAL

MEANWHILE, in far away Chicago, something of importance to the little company had taken place. The soap had begun to sell. One demand after another had come in, and finally made an impression. It was as if a stone had been dropped in the puddle and the circles had widened out and out. The last ripple reached New York and Mr. Martin when Johnson came one day to the library and announced:

"I beg pardon. A gentleman to see you, sir," handing his master a card on a silver tray.

"Mr. Charles Bronson," read Martin; "what's he want?"

"He says he's from Marshall Field, Chicago," said Johnson.

"Oh, a kick, I suppose. Send him in."

He had to confess, however, that Mr. Bronson of Chicago did not look like a kick when he came in, though his first words were ominous.

Mr. Bronson of Chicago was one of those smooth-faced, well-groomed, business men who come in hordes out of the West at certain intervals, at the time of the automobile show, for instance, and stop at the big hotels with or without their wives. Some of the maître d'hotels of New York's largest caravanserais are said to be clairvoyant on this latter point. Their greeting, "Are you alone this trip?" when the Westerner swells into the dining-room, means really: "Have you left your wife behind you?" And strangely enough, if he has, the maître d'hotel gets larger tips. But to-day, with Mr. Martin, this Mr. Bronson seemed very full of business and his business, it seemed, was about 13 Soap.

"Well, what about it?" Mr. Martin demanded, not too graciously.

Mr. Bronson took his cue and was off. While of course they understand that the 13 Soap was made by Mr. Martin's son, Mr. Rodney Martin, at the same time, as he wired he would be responsible for that order, Marshall Field felt that some one should first see him in the matter. They realized, of course, that Mr. Martin was backing his son.

"Well, why shouldn't I back him?" interrupted Martin gruffly.

"Of course, of course," Bronson agreed. "That is why we'd like to place our order through you."

Mr. Martin paused with his cigar in mid air.

"Place your what?" he repeated in amazement as he beheld Mr. Bronson snap back the elastic from his russet leather order pad and hold his pencil over it.

"Through some error we received only five thousand cakes," explained Bronson, "instead of fifty thousand; but that's all gone."

"All gone? What happened to it?"

"We've sold it."

Mr. Martin could not believe his ears.

"Sold it!" he ejaculated.

"Yes, and we want the balance of the original order you were kind enough to throw our way, and as much more soap as we can get," went on Mr. Bronson briskly.

Mr. Martin could not understand it.

"But only the other day I had a letter from Marshall Field saying they hadn't sold a cake," he said, puzzled.

Mr. Bronson laughed.

"I know, I know," he said. "We felt at first that of course there could be no popular market usual conservative publicity, well, the sales began immediately; we sold the five thousand cakes in two days."

"And the advertising did it?" Mr. Martin ventured to inquire.

"Of course, what else?" said Bronson. He proceeded with further explanations. "Now we want to handle your goods exclusively in the West, with extensive immediate deliveries. Can that be arranged?"

The soap king paused a moment to reflect.

"It ought to be. What do you offer?" he said.

"I dare say we would contract for a quarter of a million cakes of soap," began Bronson glibly.

"A quarter of a million!" repeated Martin in an astonishment which Mr. Bronson evidently misunderstood, for he added:

"Of course we might do a little better if we could settle the matter at once."

"I should have to consult my son first," said Mr. Martin at last, quite truthfully.

"Oh, then perhaps I ought to go see him," said Mr. Bronson, rising. Mr. Martin rose also.

"Not at all — not at all. I'll attend to it," he said.

"But we thought that you would have full power," began Bronson, puzzled.

"As a matter of courtesy," Mr. Martin explained, "I should like to talk things over with my own boy."

"But you control the product?"

"Mr. Bronson, you can trust me to handle this thing."

"Of course, of course; when can I see you again?"

"In half an hour," Mr. Martin answered.

"Very well," said Mr. Bronson. "I've some matters to attend to. I'll be back in half an hour. It's a wonderful soap, Mr. Martin," he vouchsafed as he went out.

"Oh, wonderful," agreed Mr. Martin dryly, watching Mr. Bronson go.

A wonderful soap indeed; plain pink castile. But he would have to get in on this. He stepped hastily to the telephone.

"1313 Worth — Hello, is this the 13 Soap Company?" he shouted in the receiver. "Just a minute. Is Mr. Rodney Martin in? No? Never mind who I am. Goodbye. Johnson," he added as the butler appeared again, "call up my son's office every ten minutes and let me know the minute he comes in. Don't tell 'em who's calling."

"Yes, sir," said Johnson docilely.

"And when Mr. Bronson comes back, be sure to have him wait for me."

"Yes, sir," said Johnson. "There's a lady to see you, sir. She speaks English now."

"She does, eh?" said Mr. Martin. "That's unusual, isn't it?"

"I mean, sir," said Johnson, "when she was here two months ago she could only talk French."

"Indeed. Well, I'm not interested in the languages she speaks. Who is she — what does she want?"

"She wishes to see you about the French rights of the 13 Soap," said Johnson.

"The what?" echoed Mr. Martin.

"The French rights," repeated Johnson.

"Great Scott — send her right in," replied his master.

"Yes, sir."

He went out immediately and re-entered, followed by the Countess gowned as usual in a charming frock and very fluent in her line of talk.

"The Countess de Bowreen," said Johnson.

Paris and Chicago met that afternoon in the library.

"How do you do?" began the clever Countess, still at her games.

"How do you do?" said Mr. Martin politely.

"I am the Countess de Beaurien. Your son have told you of me?"

"No,"

"I bet he have not. He is a cheat — he trick me."

Well, well, thought Rodney's father: this was serious.

"Now, my dear lady," he began.

"Attendez, you listen to me," the Countess rattled on. . . "Two months ago, I buy the French rights for the 13 Soap. I pay him fifteen thousand dollar and now I cannot get any soap."

"You will have to see my son," said Martin, rather disgusted.

"But I have seen him," shrieked the Countess, "and he give me no satisfaction. If I cannot get any soap, I must have my money, one or the other or I put him in the jail. He is a cheat. I have here ze contract. I sue him in the court."

"My dear lady, you mustn't feel that way," said Martin, trying to soothe her.

"Feel! Ah, mon dieu," she cried. "I trick no one, I play fair, I am an honest woman." And she went off into a long speech in French at the

"Pardon, Monsieur," said the Countess; "always when I am excited I speak the French. But! if you love your son, you pay me back, or else he go to jail. What you say?"

"But fifteen thousand dollars is a lot of money," remonstrated the soap king, too acute of course to give in at once.

"Yes. But it is more to me than it is to you," argued the lady. "You pay me, or he go to prison. Now what you say?"

At this crucial moment Ambrose Peale made his entrance, and old Martin for once in his life was glad to read his name on the card in Johnson's tray.

"By George, just the man I want to see," he said, in great relief, but fortunately not mentioning Peale's name aloud. "Show him right in. Hold on, hold on. Now, Duchess, if you don't mind, just step into this room a minute," he added, showing the unwelcome lady of title out through a door on the left.

"Very well," said the lady. "I go. I wait. But in fifteen minutes, if I do not get the fifteen thousand dollars, I go to my lawyers and your son — poof! he is done."

Meanwhile Mr. Martin turned to Johnson.

"Did you get my son's office?" he asked.

"Yes, sir — he hasn't come in yet," said Johnson.

"If you reach him while Mr. Peale's here don't mention Rodney's name; just call him 'that party.' I'll understand."

"Yes, sir."

Peale entered, and he and the soap king struck fire almost at once.

"Now see here, young man," began Martin, quite indignant at the Countess's story.

"Now one moment, Mr. Martin," Peale began. "I just want to say that I am a man of a few words. This isn't advertising — it's personal. I know you don't like me."

"Why do you say that?" Martin asked curiously.

tional scene. But when it came at last, after all his pondering and planning, it seemed very flat and unimportant. And for the life of him he could not have told how the old magnate was taking it.

"You're not a partner?" the soap king asked him at last.

"I should say not. I'm just a hired hand. He could can me any moment, but he's not the kind of guy who'd do that —"

"Then you haven't power to sign — to make a deal —"

"I should say not," said Peale. "Why, he and Miss Grayson do all the signing. If I could have signed contracts, I'd have spent a million dollars, in advertising. And, believe me, you ought to back him, because honest, Mr. Martin, it's a great scheme — the 13 Soap. On the level, if it's handled right and the publicity end is —"

"Now don't get started on advertising," Martin interposed, holding up his hand.

"That's right too," said Ambrose lamely. "Well, I guess that's all. I wanted to tell you how I stood about Rodney. That's off my chest, so good afternoon."

Mr. Martin gave a good look at this young man, who was willing to sacrifice himself for Rodney, but outwardly he did not relent.

"Wait a minute," he said presently. "What

"Have a cigar?" asked Martin.

did you boys mean by trimming that poor Countess on the French rights?"

"Jumping Jupiter, has she been here?" asked Peale, again alert.

Mr. Martin explained that she was here now, that she said she'd put Rodney in jail for fraud unless Mr. Martin made good that fifteen thousand dollars.

"I've got to pay her — can't see the boy disgraced," he concluded.

"Say, if you'd like to save that fifteen thousand dollars — I'll fix it for you," spoke up Peale.

"But she's got a contract," said Mr. Martin.

"I'll get it for you cheap," Peale answered him. "Pardon me, sir, but I know how to handle dames like her."

Mr. Martin looked at him again. Ambrose's mission had succeeded in a way he did not suspect.

"Mr. Peale, I like you," said old Martin.

"Huh?" said Peale.

"Have a cigar?" asked Martin.

Ambrose took it, feeling better than he had felt for many days. Confession is good for the soul, and self-sacrifice sometimes helps one's self. He bit his cigar and stuck his hands in his trousers pockets, strutting up and down comfortably. His feet hit the thick rug that covered the soap king's floor with a satisfactory sensation that mounted upward. On the whole Ambrose Peale felt a good deal better.

He wondered idly what that butler guy meant presently when he stuck his head in and announced to his master that he had telephoned that party, who was at his office now. He heard Martin mutter:

"Good, good. Peale, I've got to go out on an important soap deal. Oh, by George, I nearly forgot," he added. "There's another matter I must attend to first. Peale, you'll find the Countess in there — do the best you can. We'll settle the details when I get back. Make yourself at home."

"Sure. This cigar's great company," said Peale.

"Good cigar, eh?"

"Corker."

"Johnson," said Mr. Martin, "send over half a dozen boxes of those cigars to Mr. Peale's house."

"Say, Johnson," said Peale, as Mr. Martin went out, "wrap 'em up now and I'll take 'em with me."

It was a very pleasant, comfortable world, thought Ambrose. He was enjoying his cigar. He had the prospect of many good cigars out of that box Johnson was wrapping up and the re-trospect of a good impression made on Rodney's father. It was a relief to know he was not a handicap to the boy. He strutted up and down cockily on the thick rug.

Presently the telephone rang. Peale looked at it. It rang again, and he went over to the desk and raised the receiver:

"Yes, Sweetie — this is the garage. How long does it take to go to Coney Island? How in hell do I know?"

Ambrose was himself again.

But he must attend to the Countess, he re-membered, and no fooling. So he went over to the door behind which she was hiding, and threw it open with a flourish of fake French.

"Countess de Bull Run," he rattled on. "De juie — de joie — politern noblesse oblige."

The Countess came in demurely.

"You ought to take up French, Ambrose," she said sweetly; "your accent's immense. Well, little sweetheart—"

"Say, what are you doing in these parts?" Peale interrupted her.

"Oh, I came to see Mr. Martin," she said lightly.

"What for?"

"What do you think?"

"See here now, if you're aiming to trim the old man I won't stand for it," protested Ambrose.

"Ambrose, do me another favor," the Countess begged.

"What is it?"

"Don't tell old Martin what I tried to do to you boys. He's the kind that would put me in jail. I'll be on the level. I did come here to try to trim him, but I'll cut it out. Honest, I will. Oh, Ambrose, I don't like being a grafter."

"Nix, nix," said Peale.

"He left me here to settle it. Where's the contract? Come on — gimme — gimme —"

"You mean you've been on all the time?" cried the Countess.

"Sure."

"And you let me sit there a-moultin' all over the place again?"

"Gimme — gimme —"

"Oh, I suppose I've got to. Oh, I'm sick of soap anyhow. Thirteen may be lucky for you boys, but it has been a hoodoo for me."

She handed over the contract to him gracefully enough.

"And now, my little Hearts of Lettuce," Peale chanted, "this concludes your portion of the evening's entertainment."

"But at that, don't give me away, will you?" the girl pleaded.

Ambrose looked at her curiously, wondering, though he did not say so, just how to take her. He wasn't sure there wasn't some good in her for all her play acting. She attracted him. He treasured her address. He didn't relish playing second fiddle to Ellery Clark, but he kept the address. He didn't believe Ellery would last, with all his money, and the address might come handy. But aloud all he would say was:

"I like you. You've got brains. Most chickens are just chickens."

"And you are an eighteen karat kid," said the Countess. "Ta — ta," she added. "Ring me up some day."

"So long," said Ambrose. "Be good."

And so he assisted at the dismissal of one of Mr. Martin's callers that afternoon. Of the first, of Mr. Bronson of Chicago and his fifty thousand cakes, he had not heard yet. Perhaps this was just as well; the mood of Ambrose this Saturday afternoon had grown far too genial anyway.

Into the middle of this mood, just as he was showing the Countess to the door, with no intervention by the faithful Johnson, burst Mary, followed by Rodney in a tearing hurry. They stopped abruptly when they saw Ambrose.

"Oh, have you seen father?" Rodney asked. "Is he here?"

"I'm waiting for him now," Peale answered.

"It's most important," said Mary breathlessly.

"You remember the Countess," Peale put in cautiously.

They all bowed, embarrassed, and there was an awkward pause, which the Countess broke.

"Well, I guess I'm not wanted," she said perspicaciously, looking shrewdly at the trio, "so I'll trot. I'll trot. So long, you 13 soap-suds."

CHAPTER XVI

A WEDDING

CHAPTER XVI

A WEDDING

ALAS for the inequalities of this world! If for Ambrose Peale these last days had been blue, for Rodney and Mary they had been all the color of roses.

Much history had passed over their heads as well as the company's in the hours leading up to their visit to Mr. Martin's library, and their foregathering there with Ambrose and the Countess. The order from Marshall Field had begun it, and that was really the soap king's fault, since he had waved his monopolistic wand and caused the false order to spring up out of the ground: and Mary's five thousand dollar contribution to the soap company's capital had developed it, which may also be said to have been the fault of the old magnate. The Marshall Field order was especially to blame, however, because it had made the future look assured and rosy and encouraging, so that together they had taken the plunge. In the illuminated moments which followed the fifty-thousand flash Mary's reluctance had disappeared, Rodney's ardor had redoubled and in the reaction of a lovers' quarrel and a "grand make-up" as Mary said, they had gone off to the Little Church around the corner and been married. That was the whole story. Really and truly it was all old Mr. Martin's fault, and prearranged by him from the beginning, as Mary told herself again and again, defending herself against Rodney's father's possible wrath when the news of his son's marriage to a typewriter should be broken gently to him.

The quarrel came, as quarrels and April showers are apt to do, out of a clear and serene sky. In the general jubilation over Marshall Field Rodney had remarked, escorting Mary up town at night, that now, the first thing he was going to do with his share of the profits, was to pay her back that five thousand dollars.

"And then," he added sententiously, "there won't be anything between us any more."

Something in the tone of his voice, quite unintentional on the boy's part, no doubt, had piqued Mary.

"You've always fussed about that," she said.

Something in the way she said the word fussed piqued Rodney.

"And don't you think it's been something to fuss about?" he demanded. "When a fellow's best girl, his fiancée, takes money from a rich old man, and then the fellow lets her lose it all in his business — well, I don't see why you can't see that the situation's pretty raw."

"Why do you say lost? I hope you don't think it's really lost," retorted Mary. "Don't be such a gloomy Gus."

"Well, you know what I mean," persisted Rodney. "It was darned near lost. And that shows you do care about it any way."

"Why shouldn't I care about it?" said Mary. "Indeed I think five thousand dollars is a good deal of money."

"I think it's a whole lot of money," said Rodney, "and you must excuse me if I can't help wondering how a girl in your position was able to get hold of it."

"A girl in my position," echoed Mary scornfully. "That's right. Rub it in. I'm really ashamed of you, Rodney Martin. And you know perfectly well I wasn't born a typewriter."

She turned her head away and there was just a hint of tears in her voice, but Rodney was not ready to give in yet. He was bent, masculine fashion, on making her listen to reason, as if the matter were the most important in the world, and he thought he saw his chance at last to get the truth about it out of her.

"Mary," he said, trying to be perfectly calm

and persuasive, "tell me now. You know we shall be happier."

"I don't know it at all," said Mary obstinately.

They had left the subway now, and were walking east in the long block toward Central Park. When they came to the stoop of Mary's house they both paused and Rodney began to plead again.

"Mary, please," he said, trying to take her hand.

"No," said Mary, "I don't believe you'd like me if you knew."

"Please," persisted Rodney.

The long, uniform rows of New York house fronts stretched away on either side of them in the obscurity. A red light twinkled in one bay window, and beneath the shade could be seen the rows of books in a library. Near the curb opposite an extraordinarily silent limousine had just drawn up, with a little swish of its rubber tires as it came to rest, and presently a man and a woman in joyous evening raiment came out of the house and got into it. The woman wore a perfectly gorgeous opera cloak and combs flashed in her beautifully arranged hair. The man's linen was very white and his silk hat very shiny. The chauffeur had switched on the light inside the car, and the occupants showed a moment brilliantly in the jewel box of its interior, before the light went out and the car moved off again, west and south, to the haunts of pleasure, as Ambrose Peale would have said. A throb and a sob came into Mary's voice as she saw it all, and she answered again:

"You might hate me. And I'm taking you away from all that, which was yours by right."

"Come in a moment," said Rodney, gently and kindly. "As if I cared. You know nothing can ever make any difference to me. I only want to know where I am, that's all."

They climbed the stairs together and a West Indian "butler" let them in. Rodney drew Mary into a hideous little reception-room on the ground floor, and they sat down together on a Turkish couch which bore a suspicious suggestion of being a disguised bed. He took both the girl's hands in his and looked earnestly into her lovely eyes.

"You're the finest girl in the world, Mary," he said, "and nothing could ever turn me against you."

In the ill-lighted, ill-ventilated little parlor, illuminated for them with love's thousand eyes, the truth came out. Mary told the whole story from the beginning, not without some humor, and not without some satisfaction at certain portions of it, it must be confessed; told of old Mr. Martin's fretting about Ellery Clark, of the bet with Ellery's father, of her share in the deception and of her reward in money.

"But you see I believed in you, Rodney," she concluded, "and so I reinvested in your business."

"What do I care, if you really love me," protested Rodney. "And you must prove it too. Mary, now you must marry me."

Between the lines of her story Rodney had read real and growing love for him; she had really learned to love him, he told himself jubilantly, and he thrilled with the wonder of it. It had been worth working for. He was a man now, full grown, and he took her in his arms and pressed his lips to hers, and gathered her sweet, slim yielding body to his in a long, passionate embrace —

That was a Thursday, and by Friday night they were married; so that they could have two days of honeymoon any way before Monday, Rodney said. It was all very quietly arranged in the little church. English sparrows chirped noisily in the bare branches of the churchyard, and the little fountain, its waters frozen till it took the shape of the cut on an old apollinaris bottle, trickled gently, as they passed in. When they came out nothing was visible to Rodney except the lovelight in Mary's eyes. . . .

So much for those who talk about telepathy.

Late Saturday forenoon, when they sneaked down to the office, just to be sure that everything was all right, certainly no one guessed what momentous change had come into their two lives; no one divined the ecstasy that thrilled unseen beneath their every day demeanor. Miss Burke, watching Mary take off her hat and pat back her hair, and Rodney hanging up his coat, had not the slightest idea of anything so romantic.

Of course old Mr. Martin's obduracy had been a blow, but Rodney was game throughout, and gloriously happy. He felt every inch a man now, and dared to cope with every difficulty.

"Shall we tell the old gentleman?" he asked Mary, meaning of course the fact of their being married.

"No, indeed, not yet," said Mary, blushing ever so little. "Just let me wait for the psychological moment."

So they waited, and love was rewarded once more by nothing less ethereal than a second order for soap that very morning. It was from Gimbel's, and this time they simply must fill it. They both agreed; wherefore they had flown at once to Mr. Martin's house, in the midst of their honeymoon.

They arrived while Mr. Bronson of Chicago was putting in his half hour wait by feeding peanuts to the chipmunks in Central Park. They found only Ambrose there, though very much at home; and Ambrose, of course, once the Countess was disposed of, wanted to know what the excitement was all about. Mary told him. It seemed that just after they got to the office that morning a letter from Gimbel's had come in.

"Ordering ten thousand cakes of 13 Soap," interrupted Rodney.

"Now what do you think of that?" said Mary.

"Pinch me — I'm dreaming," Peale told her.

"They say our advertising's wonderful," went on Rodney, "and has created such a demand they want to handle the soap in town."

Peale did actually pinch himself in the flesh this time, convinced that he must wake up before he set his heart on finding things true. He pinched himself so hard he said "Ouch," and then he whistled, long and wonderingly.

"By Jimminy, then all the things we told your father the other day are really true," he said.

"Of course they are," declared Mary.

"Gosh," said Peale.

Rodney went on:

"You see when I show father this letter from Gimbel, he's got to admit we've won out — and supply us with soap."

"Isn't it a shame that you can't get soap from anybody but him?" pouted Mary.

"Father certainly has got the soap business tied up tight," said Rodney.

"Yes, if he busted the whole world would go dirty," laughed Peale.

"Suppose he's still stubborn and won't help us, what shall we do?" asked Mary.

"Oh, we'll just have to plod along," said Rodney.

"Don't plod — gallop, son — gallop — gallop," amended Peale, full of his high spirits.

Rodney looked meaningly at Mary and then at Peale.

"You're a great pal, old man," he said, and Mary added:

"Do you know, Mr. Peale, I like you awfully?"

Peale looked quickly at each to see if they were chaffing, and then winked broadly.

"Call me Ambrose," he said demurely, to Mary, trying to make Rodney jealous.

"Ambrose," said Mary coyly.

"If we ever do come out of this you're going to be my partner, fifty to fifty," declared Rodney, feeling not jealous, but kind to all the world.

"Aw shut up," said Peale.

"Mr. Charles Bronson; shall I show him in?" said Johnson, in the doorway.

"You have my permission — this isn't my house," said Peale promptly.

"Oh, I beg pardon — I expected to find Mr. Martin," said Mr. Bronson, stepping briskly into the room.

"I am Mr. Martin," spoke up Rodney.

"Mr. Rodney Martin?" pursued Bronson eagerly.

"Yes," said Rodney.

"Just the very man I wanted to see — on private business," said Bronson.

"Oh, these are my partners," said Rodney. "You can talk before them. This is Mr. Peale and Miss Grayson." There was just a shade of hesitation as he called Mary, Miss Grayson. "May I present — Mr. —"

"Charles Bronson of Marshall Field."

"Marshall Field?" said Rodney, amazed.

"Marshall Field?" cried Mary.

"Marshall Field?" echoed Peale.

The man from Chicago went straight on with his errand.

"Now about your soap?"

"Now see here, old man," protested Rodney, disarming criticism.

"Oh Lord," thought Peale, then added aloud, politely, "We're very sorry—"

"Indeed we are," chimed in Mary, "but a bargain is a bargain."

Mr. Bronson looked at the three in a kind of busy wonder.

"Sorry?" he said. "Why, your 13 Soap the last few days has had a most remarkable sale at our store in Chicago."

Mary and Peale, speechless, looked at each other blankly. Rodney gasped:

"You mean it is realy selling?"

"Rather," said Bronson.

"It's really selling?" Mary echoed.

"Why—you seem surprised," said Bronson, studying their faces.

Mary pulled herself together briskly, the first of them all.

"Oh, not—not a bit," she repudiated.

"Oh, not a bit," said Rodney.

But Peale still longed to know the whole truth at last.

"You mean people are actually coming into the store and buying it?" he went on.

"At a dollar a cake," said Bronson.

"It was those page advertisements in Chicago that did it," conceded Mary.

"Absolutely," said Peale.

Extraordinary advertisements they were too, in

Bronson's opinion, though nothing to what Rodney assured him they would do in the near future. Mr. Bronson nodded complacently, and wanted to know if they would keep up their campaign; that would have some bearing, of course, on the subject in hand.

"Double it," said Rodney.

"Triple it," said Peale from the bottom of his heart.

"Good, good," said Mr. Bronson. "We foresee a tremendous sale for your goods. It's an amazing soap. Do you control the company yourself?"

"Oh, entirely," said Rodney.

"Then I can deal with you," Bronson began again.

"With us — all of us," Rodney asserted, and Bronson went on:

"We should be glad to contract now for two hundred and fifty thousand cakes—"

Peale just flopped into a chair—

"With deliveries to begin next week."

Mary, whose brain had been going like lightning, now took a hand. She went and stood near Rodney, as if to control the situation better.

"Our capacity just at present is limited," she said, cautiously.

" Yes, we have so many orders on hand," agreed Rodney.

" Naturally, but how much soap can you deliver now ? " inquired Bronson.

" I don't quite know," said Rodney. " Do you ? " he added, turning to Peale.

" Not quite," said Peale, turning to Mary, " do you ? "

" Not quite," said Mary, with regretful visions of her " factory."

" Well, under the circumstances, what can we do ? " said Bronson.

" That's the question," Rodney agreed.

" What's the answer ? " speculated Peale.

Meanwhile Rodney's brain had been working too.

" Here's an idea," he said, " in view of our press of orders ; would you entertain the idea of paying us merely for the use of our trademark, without any soap at all ? "

" Yes, I think we would," Bronson said, considering a moment. " Your trademark is of course your biggest asset. You would naturally give us your formula ? "

" Yes, if we still have that cook book," blurted Peale.

" I beg pardon," said Bronson.

"Nothing, nothing. Have a cigar," said Peale.

"I've got the cook book," said Mary.

"You can have the formula," Rodney agreed.

Mr. Bronson cleared his throat and went on:

"With a license from you to use the title, I dare say we could arrange to have the soap manufactured by Cyrus Martin of the Soap Trust."

"How much would you pay for the trademark?" put in Mary.

"I should have to call up our Chicago office," said Bronson; "but I think I can safely say we should be prepared to offer you at least two hundred and fifty thousand dollars."

Peale gasped, but controlled himself in time to say "Indeed," in a very genteel tone of voice.

"Can I have an option at that figure?" pursued Bronson.

"No!" said Mary.

"Yes!" said Peale.

"Yes!" said Rodney.

"No," said Mary again, loudly and resolutely.

"No," said Rodney, following her lead.

"No — but I hate to say it," wound up Peale.

"And so do I," said Rodney.

"But if you control the company, why not settle matters now?" began Bronson.

"Why not, Mary?" asked Rodney.

" Yes, why not, Mary? " inquired Peale.

Mary threw Rodney a meaning look and Peale caught it on the fly.

" Hadn't we better discuss the matter a little more fully first among ourselves? " she said sweetly.

" Yes," said Mr. Bronson tactfully; " perhaps I could wait somewhere for a few minutes while you talk things over."

" Yes, do please — in the next room," suggested Mary.

Mr. Bronson took up his hat and stepped to the door.

" I am very glad to have met you," he said.

" Not half as glad," began Rodney.

" Not half as glad," began Peale.

"— not half as glad as we are to have met you," finished Mary.

" No, not half as much," said Peale, and could hardly keep from cheering and capering behind Bronson's back.

Mary and Rodney looked at each other as if they thought life very well worth while.

CHAPTER XVII

A WEDDING PRESENT

CHAPTER XVII

A WEDDING PRESENT

THE door had no sooner closed on Mr. Bronson than the board of directors of the 13 Soap Company went into immediate and special session. Rodney and Peale both pounced on Mary, Peale half-vexed, and Rodney very curious.

"Why not give him an option at a quarter of a million?"

"Yes, why not — for the love of geewhiz tell us that?"

But Mary stood her ground.

"Because maybe we can get more money than that out of your father," she said quietly.

Rodney kissed her right in the meeting and Peale coughed.

"Mary, you are a wonder," he said.

"Gosh, I wish you were going to marry me," said Peale.

Mary said nothing, for at that moment she spied Johnson coming up, and the sight of him helped give her an idea.

"Johnson, oh, Johnson — you know I've always liked you," she began, attracting his attention vehemently.

"I beg pardon, Miss?"

"Will you do me a favor?" she went on.

"Why, yes, Miss —"

"When Mr. Martin comes back don't tell him that Rodney and Mr. Peale are here, or Bronson either. Say I'm alone."

"Yes, Miss, but Mr. Martin has just driven up in his car; he'll be here directly —"

"Hurry up, then. Tell him I'm here, waiting for him," said Mary.

Johnson went out obediently.

"But I don't understand," Rodney expostulated.

"Neither do I," said Peale.

"I do," said Mary, who sounded as if she knew exactly what she was about. "I've got a great idea. You two boys go into that room and stay there. Now listen. Keep Bronson there. When I ring this buzzer twice, you call me on this phone — there's a switch in there — and never mind what I say.— Now hurry up, both of you. I'm going to try to make a deal with your father."

Peale chirped up at once.

"Well," he said, patting his breast pocket, "I'll slip you something that may help you when you see father. You tell him that I've got that contract. He'll understand."

" But I don't know what any of this is about," protested Rodney, finding the situation more and more complex.

" Neither do I," said Peale. " Come on; she's got more brains than both of us."

They went out reluctantly and Mary settled herself comfortably in an armchair to wait for Mr. Martin.

As a matter of fact she was a little ashamed of what she proposed to do, but was arguing stubbornly with herself that it was all right, that Mr. Martin would agree with her, when he heard all and knew all that she did. In this predatory world of business you had to look out for yourself. It seemed a very predatory world indeed as she looked back over the recent episodes of her life; — everybody was trying to do everybody else — Mr. Martin " doing " Mr. Clark, the Soap Company doing Mr. Martin, the Countess doing whom she could, and Peale doing the whole world with his advertising. Of course the Countess was a real crook; Mary only hoped Ambrose would reform her, and she had an idea he would, that things were drifting that way. The rest was just business. Business was business. And Mr. Martin's money was all in the family, so to speak.

Mr. Martin himself came in on her revery.

"Hello, Miss Grayson," he said, seeing her; "this is another pleasant surprise. Where is Rodney?"

He sounded as if he wanted to see the boy really.

"That doesn't matter. I'm here," said Mary demurely.

Mr. Martin looked round for Bronson and Peale.

"Where's that — that Mr.—" he began.

"Mr. Peale?" said Mary. "Oh, Mr. Peale's gone back to the office; but he told me to tell you that he'd got that contract —"

"Oh, he did, did he?" said Martin. "Great, great; he's a smart boy."

"We are all smart," said Mary; "it's a smart firm. We've just got a letter from Gimbels for ten thousand cakes of 13 Soap, and this time you didn't send the telegram —"

Mr. Martin took this news with complete good nature.

"Gimbels, eh? Well, well. Now I'll be frank," he said. "I want Rodney to come in with me — and you've got to help. You started this scheme. Now finish it up."

"What's changed you all of a sudden?" asked Mary.

"The board of directors of the 13 Soap Company."

"Well, Gimbels, for one thing," said the old gentleman. "That shows sensational advertising does pay. Those boys are right. I've been too conservative; but anyhow I've got the whip hand. Rodney can't get his soap for Gimbels except from me, and if I'm going to furnish three cent soap that he sells wholesale for sixty cents, I'm going to be in on the profits. Any young man who can do that is just bound to have me for a partner, whether he wants me or not. What do you say, Miss Grayson?"

"I'll do all I can for Rodney," said Mary, looking down.

"You have authority to close the deal?" asked Mr. Martin.

"Absolutely," said Mary.

"Good. Now what's your proposition?" he inquired, sitting down.

"Five hundred thousand dollars cash," said Mary quietly.

"What!" yelled Mr. Martin, jumping out of his chair.

Mary went on calmly:

"Sit down. That isn't all. We are to get fifty-one per cent. of the stock, you put up a factory and give Rodney fifty thousand a year, Peale forty thousand, and me twenty thousand."

Mr. Martin took a good look at her and whistled.

"As my son once observed, what lovely weather we're having," he said. He leant back and lighted a cigar, and as he did so Mary pushed the buzzer twice. Almost instantly the telephone rang.

"Shall I answer it?" said Mary politely.

"Go ahead — say I'm out," Martin grunted.

"Oh, hello," said Mary in the telephone, adding in an aside to Mr. Martin, "it's for me. Hello, Rodney — you've seen Bronson?"

"Bronson?" repeated Mr. Martin, sitting up.

"He did?" said Mary in the telephone; "why, that's a splendid offer. I hardly dared think Marshall Field would be so generous."

"I'll accept your proposition, Miss Grayson," interrupted Mr. Martin hastily.

"Wait," said Mary. "Have you closed with Bronson yet?" she went on to the mouthpiece. "Oh, you haven't?"

"Good," grunted Mr. Martin, listening.

"No," Mary went on, "I think you'd better come right up from the office and see me before you sign anything."

Mr. Martin strode over to her quickly.

"Here, let me talk to him," he said, and reached for the phone.

"Oh, hello, hello," called Mary quickly and jiggled the bell. "Oh dear, we've been cut off. Still, it doesn't matter — it's all settled now."

"That's splendid, Miss Grayson. I'm grateful to you," said Mr. Martin.

"Shall we sign a memorandum now?" asked Mary a little nervously.

"Sure — sure — just the rough details," he agreed.

"Sure, never put off till to-morrow what you can sign to-day," said Mary, smiling reminiscently.

Mr. Martin sat down at his desk and began to write:

"Fifty-one per cent.— Rodney — fifty thousand — And what's that young man's name again — Spiel?"

"Peale," said Mary.

"That certainly is one hell of a name — thirty thousand — Grayson twenty thousand — there." Then to Mary: "You sign here."

"No, you sign first," said Mary.

Mr. Martin grunted and signed.

"Now I'll sign for Rodney," said Mary, and did so gleefully.

"That's great," said Mr. Martin.

"You don't know how great it is," assented Mary, and started for the door. "Now I've a big surprise for you. Rodney's not at the office — he's in there."

"What do you mean?"

"Only that I thought I'd handle you less sentimentally than he would. You see once before I spoiled Rodney's plan. This time I thought I ought to fix it up for him. Rodney, Ambrose," she called, throwing the door open.

"Say, what is all this?" Martin exclaimed, as Rodney and Peale came in.

"Rodney, it's all settled," Mary began. "Your father has come in with us. I've the contract."

"Then we can get some soap?" asked Rodney.

"All you want," said Martin.

"Then I don't care what the arrangement is," cried Rodney; "now that we can make good. Twenty per cent. of the profits, and any old salary."

"Twenty per cent., why, she buncoed me out of fifty-one per cent. and half a million down," growled his father.

"Half a million!" gasped Peale.

"You did?" asked Rodney. "Mary, you are a wonder."

"Absolutely," said Peale.

But Mary was not quite through yet. She turned to Mr. Martin again and said:

"And by the terms of my contract with you, you now owe me ten per cent. of what Rodney has made — fifty thousand dollars."

"What contract?" asked Rodney curiously.

Mr. Martin growled and snorted.

"So that's why you held me up, eh?" he sputtered. "Just to get your ten per cent. Say, young lady, I've got a lot of other money that you are overlooking."

"Father, what do you mean?" Rodney persisted.

"I'll tell you what I mean," said his father. "She got engaged to you to make you go to work — She only left me to keep you on the job because I promised her ten per cent. of what you earned. All the time that she's been pretending she would marry you she's been making use of you."

"Mary, you did this to me?" Rodney asked.

"I don't believe it," Peale declared.

"You owe me fifty thousand dollars — can I have the check, please?" said Mary quietly to Mr. Martin.

"Yes," said the soap king, "if you'll quit now — get out of here for good. I'm disappointed to think you'd treat my boy like this."

"What's the difference?" asked Mary. "If

I'd really loved him you'd have objected to his marrying only a typewriter."

"Objected! If you'd been on the level I'd have been proud to have you for my daughter," said the father, handing his check to Rodney.

"Hurrah, Mary, it's all right now."

"I don't get you," said Peale.

"What is this — a joke?" said Martin.

"Certainly it is — you put up a joke on Mary and me, and I thought we'd put up one for you. Mary has told me about that contract already."

"You mean you're going to marry her?" asked his father.

"Certainly not," said Rodney, trying not to smile.

"Why aren't you going to marry her?" demanded Martin.

"Because we are married already — married yesterday," said Rodney proudly.

Peale looked at his two partners, and actually blushed with surprise at this astounding news.

"And we thought before we told you of our marriage," went on Rodney, "we'd get her percentage for a wedding present."

"And it's bigger than we ever hoped for," added Mary.

Mr. Martin opened his mouth and whistled.

"By George, you boys were right — I am an old fool. Anyhow, I'll win that bet from old John Clark."

"And now for Mr. Bronson," said Mary, still in quiet control of the situation, opening the door for Bronson to come in.

"You boys know Bronson?" asked Mr. Martin.

"Oh, yes," said Mary; "we had a long talk with him, right in this room, about a proposition from Marshall Field. You talk to him, father."

"Yes, father, you talk to him," said Peale.

Mr. Bronson turned to Rodney.

"But I thought I was dealing with you,—"

"No, sir, with me — now what's your proposition?" demanded the soap king.

"A quarter of a million cash just for the trade-mark," said Bronson.

"A quarter of a million?" said Martin scornfully to the quailing Bronson. "Why, you ought to be ashamed of yourself to try to trim these poor boys like that."

The events of his busy and momentous morning had been gradually mounting to old Mr. Martin's head. The excitement of putting through an important deal, the winning of the bet from John Clark, the reclamation of his boy Rodney, and finally Rodney's marriage with Mary Grayson, something he had always wanted, exhilarated him; and as wine boils up unaccustomed things in one's brain, so this last speech by Bronson caused the soap king to pour forth all the bits of advertising talk that had been flowing round him for the last six months. He squared away like Ambrose Peale, for all the world, and let Bronson have a full blast.

"You know that 13 Soap is worth half a million in Chicago alone," he shouted. "And you try to take advantage of these kids' ignorance. Why, it's outrageous; but you can't trim me.— No, sir — we wouldn't take a million. Do you know that the Uneeda trademark is valued at six million, the Gold Dust Twins at ten million and our trademark is better than theirs? We're going to advertise all over the world — That's what advertising means — the power of suggestion — the psychology of print. All you have to do is to say a thing often enough and hard enough and ninety-seven per cent. of the public'll fall. Get 'em talking about you — don't let 'em be quiet — mention your name — argue about it — be a hero or a villain — but don't be a dub. Say, what kind of garters do you wear? Boston? Why? Because all your life every time you opened a magazine you saw a picture of a man's leg with a certain kind of garter on it — Boston —"

"Well, father, father," laughed Mary, hearing this torrent of advertising talk from these erstwhile "conservative" lips. "You've got religion."

"And you need it, Missy," cried the delighted soap king, turning on her.

"Mrs., if you please," laughed Mary.

"Mrs. Rodney Martin, eh?" he chuckled. "Tell me all about it all over again. When were you married? Where did you go? Where do you live? I'll tell you one thing, anyway. You've got to come and live here now, both of you."

"It's a good thing I never took away my trunk after all," said Rodney, putting one arm around Mary's waist and shaking his father's hand with the other.

Mr. Martin took out a large silk handkerchief and blew his nose quite loudly.

"I'll settle a hundred thousand dollars on the first grandchild," he said, "just for luck."

"Well, well," said Ambrose Peale, with a suspicious twinkle in his eye. "Believe me, it pays to advertise."

THE END

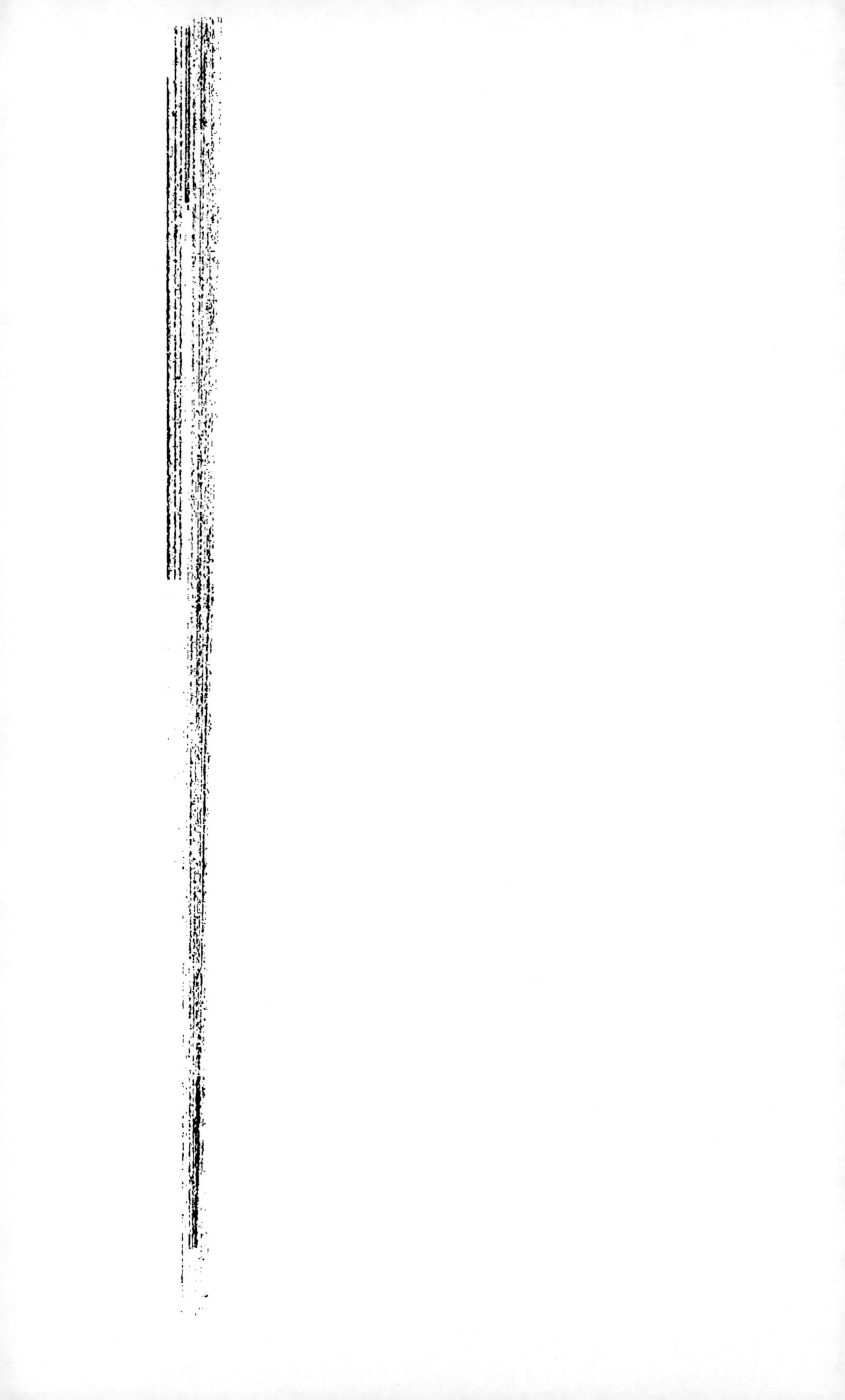

JOHN FOX, JR'S.

STORIES OF THE KENTUCKY MOUNTAINS

May be had wherever books are sold. ✻ Ask for Grosset and Dunlap's list.

THE TRAIL OF THE LONESOME PINE.

Illustrated by F. C. Yohn.

The "lonesome pine" from which the story takes its name was a tall tree that stood in solitary splendor on a mountain top. The fame of the pine lured a young engineer through Kentucky to catch the trail, and when he finally climbed to its shelter he found not only the pine but the *foot-prints of a girl.* And the girl proved to be lovely, piquant, and the trail of these girlish foot-prints led the young engineer a madder chase than "the trail of the lonesome pine."

THE LITTLE SHEPHERD OF KINGDOM COME

Illustrated by F. C. Yohn.

This is a story of Kentucky, in a settlement known as "Kingdom Come." It is a life rude, semi-barbarous; but natural and honest, from which often springs the flower of civilization.

"Chad," the "little shepherd" did not know who he was nor whence he came—he had just wandered from door to door since early childhood, seeking shelter with kindly mountaineers who gladly fathered and mothered this waif about whom there was such a mystery—a charming waif, by the way, who could play the banjo better that anyone else in the mountains.

A KNIGHT OF THE CUMBERLAND.

Illustrated by F. C. Yohn.

The scenes are laid along the waters of the Cumberland, the lair of moonshiner and feudsman. The knight is a moonshiner's son, and the heroine a beautiful girl perversely christened "The Blight." Two impetuous young Southerners' fall under the spell of "The Blight's" charms and she learns what a large part jealousy and pistols have in the love making of the mountaineers.

Included in this volume is "Hell fer-Sartain" and other stories, some of Mr. Fox's most entertaining Cumberland valley narratives.

Ask for complete free list of G. & D. Popular Copyrighted Fiction

GROSSET & DUNLAP, 526 WEST 26th ST., NEW YORK

CHARMING BOOKS FOR GIRLS

May be had wherever books are sold. Ask for Grosset & Dunlap's list

WHEN PATTY WENT TO COLLEGE, By Jean Webster.

Illustrated by C. D. Williams.

One of the best stories of life in a girl's college that has ever been written. It is bright, whimsical and entertaining, lifelike, laughable and thoroughly human.

JUST PATTY, By Jean Webster.

Illustrated by C. M. Relyea.

Patty is full of the joy of living, fun-loving, given to ingenious mischief for its own sake, with a disregard for pretty convention which is an unfailing source of joy to her fellows.

THE POOR LITTLE RICH GIRL, By Eleanor Gates.

With four full page illustrations.

This story relates the experience of one of those unfortunate children whose early days are passed in the companionship of a governess, seldom seeing either parent, and famishing for natural love and tenderness. A charming play as dramatized by the author.

REBECCA OF SUNNYBROOK FARM, By Kate Douglas Wiggin.

One of the most beautiful studies of childhood—Rebecca's artistic, unusual and quaintly charming qualities stand out midst a circle of austere New Englanders. The stage version is making a phenominal dramatic record.

NEW CHRONICLES OF REBECCA, By Kate Douglas Wiggin.

Illustrated by F. C. Yohn.

Additional episodes in the girlhood of this delightful heroine that carry Rebecca through various stages to her eighteenth birthday.

REBECCA MARY, By Annie Hamilton Donnell.

Illustrated by Elizabeth Shippen Green.

This author possesses the rare gift of portraying all the grotesque little joys and sorrows and scruples of this very small girl with a pathos that is peculiarly genuine and appealing.

EMMY LOU: Her Book and Heart, By George Madden Martin

Illustrated by Charles Louis Hinton.

Emmy Lou is irresistibly lovable, because she is so absolutely real. She is just a bewitchingly innocent, hugable little maid. The book is wonderfully human.

Ask for complete free list of G. & D. Popular Copyrighted Fiction

GROSSET & DUNLAP, 526 WEST 26th ST., NEW YORK

LOUIS TRACY'S

CAPTIVATING AND EXHILARATING ROMANCES

May be had wherever books are sold. Ask for Grosset & Dunlap's list

CYNTHIA'S CHAUFFEUR. Illustrated by Howard Chandler Christy.

A pretty American girl in London is touring in a car with a chauffeur whose identity puzzles her. An amusing mystery.

THE STOWAWAY GIRL. Illustrated by Nesbitt Benson.

A shipwreck, a lovely girl stowaway, a rascally captain, a fascinating officer, and thrilling adventures in South Seas.

THE CAPTAIN OF THE KANSAS.

Love and the salt sea, a helpless ship whirled into the hands of cannibals, desperate fighting and a tender romance.

THE MESSAGE. Illustrated by Joseph Cummings Chase.

A bit of parchment found in the figurehead of an old vessel tells of a buried treasure. A thrilling mystery develops.

THE PILLAR OF LIGHT.

The pillar thus designated was a lighthouse, and the author tells with exciting detail the terrible dilemma of its cut-off inhabitants.

THE WHEEL O'FORTUNE. With illustrations by James Montgomery Flagg.

The story deals with the finding of a papyrus containing the particulars of some of the treasures of the Queen of Sheba.

A SON OF THE IMMORTALS. Illustrated by Howard Chandler Christy.

A young American is proclaimed king of a little Balkan Kingdom, and a pretty Parisian art student is the power behind the throne.

THE WINGS OF THE MORNING.

A sort of Robinson Crusoe *redivivus* with modern settings and a very pretty love story added. The hero and heroine, are the only survivors of a wreck, and have many thrilling adventures on their desert island.

Ask for complete free list of G. & D. Popular Copyrighted Fiction

GROSSET & DUNLAP, 526 WEST 26th ST., NEW YORK